PRAISE FOR

The Becoming

"This is a really, really good book. Anna is a great character, Stein's plotting is adventurous and original, and I think most of my readers would have a great time with *The Becoming*. Best of all, Stein is writing a sequel."
—*New York Times* bestselling author Charlaine Harris

"*The Becoming* is a cross between MaryJanice Davidson's Undead series starring Betsy Taylor and Laurell K. Hamilton's Anita Blake series. She's a kick-butt bounty hunter—but vampires are a complete surprise to her. Full of interesting twists and turns that will leave readers guessing, *The Becoming* is a great addition to the TBR pile."
—*Romance Reviews Today*

"In an almost Hitchcockian way, this story keeps you guessing, with new twists and turns coming almost every page. Anna is well named, strong in ways she does not even know. There is a strong element of surprise to it . . . even if you don't like vampire novels, you ought to give this one a shot."
—*Huntress Reviews*

THE
BECOMING

JEANNE C. STEIN

ACE BOOKS, NEW YORK

THE BERKLEY PUBLISHING GROUP
Published by the Penguin Group
Penguin Group (USA) Inc.
375 Hudson Street, New York, New York 10014, USA
Penguin Group (Canada), 90 Eglinton Avenue East, Suite 700, Toronto, Ontario M4P 2Y3, Canada
(a division of Pearson Penguin Canada Inc.)
Penguin Books Ltd., 80 Strand, London WC2R 0RL, England
Penguin Group Ireland, 25 St. Stephen's Green, Dublin 2, Ireland (a division of Penguin Books Ltd.)
Penguin Group (Australia), 250 Camberwell Road, Camberwell, Victoria 3124, Australia
(a division of Pearson Australia Group Pty. Ltd.)
Penguin Books India Pvt. Ltd., 11 Community Centre, Panchsheel Park, New Delhi—110 017, India
Penguin Group (NZ), Cnr. Airborne and Rosedale Roads, Albany, Auckland 1310, New Zealand
(a division of Pearson New Zealand Ltd.)
Penguin Books (South Africa) (Pty.) Ltd., 24 Sturdee Avenue, Rosebank, Johannesburg 2196, South
Africa

Penguin Books Ltd., Registered Offices: 80 Strand, London WC2R 0RL, England

THE BECOMING

An Ace Book / published by arrangement with ImaJinn Books

PRINTING HISTORY
ImaJinn Books edition / 2004
Ace mass-market edition / December 2006

Copyright © 2004 by Jeanne C. Stein.
Permission granted to use material from: *Monsters: An Investigator's Guide to Magical Beings* by
John Michael Greer © 2001. Llewellyn Worldwide, Ltd. PO Box 64383, St. Paul, MN 55164. All
rights reserved.
Cover art by Cliff Nielsen. Cover design by Judith Lagerman.
Interior text design by Kristin del Rosario

ISBN: 0-441-01456-9

ACE
Ace Books are published by The Berkley Publishing Group,
a division of Penguin Group (USA) Inc.,
375 Hudson Street, New York, New York 10014.
ACE and the "A" design are trademarks belonging to Penguin Group (USA) Inc.

PRINTED IN THE UNITED STATES OF AMERICA

10 9 8 7 6 5 4 3 2 1

FOREWORD

MY NAME IS ANNA STRONG. I WAS THIRTY ON my last birthday, and I will be thirty when you read this. In fact, physically I will never be older than thirty no matter how many mortal years I have on this earth. I am vampire. How I became, and what is the nature of my existence, is the reason for this story. I tell it the way it happened so you will learn the truth as I did.

It may not be what you expect.

CHAPTER 1

IT'S ONE IN THE MORNING, LATE LAST JULY, AND hot. I'm squirming around on the front seat of my car like a fidgety five-year-old. I can't even keep my fingers still. As if with a mind of their own, they drum a restless tattoo on the steering wheel.

David should have had Donaldson out of that bar thirty minutes ago. What can be keeping him?

I squint around the dark parking lot. I hate waiting. I'm no good at it. You'd think after two and a half years chasing scumbags—excuse me, *alleged* scumbags—for a living, I would have developed some patience.

I haven't.

I open the car door and step out. The dampness folds around me, a combination of heat, humidity, and a stubborn fog that clings to the Southern California coast like a soggy blanket. It's too late in the season for "June gloom." What happened to real summer, with a lazy sun and warm desert air to dry things out? Instead, the humidity plasters my silk blouse to my skin. Shit, it's like living in Florida. I shake out of a linen jacket and throw in onto the front seat before slamming the car door shut.

Impatiently, I smooth wrinkles out of my skirt. I should have taken the time to change into my usual work garb—jeans and a cotton tee. Besides being downright uncomfortable, these clothes remind me that I had once again subjected myself to a less-than-perfect dinner spent trying to justify my work to my parents. For the first time in thirty years I have a business of my own and real money in the bank. I'm happy doing exactly what I want to be doing. But is that enough for them?

Apparently not.

Of course, if they saw me now, standing in a smelly alley behind a storage building in a not-so-upscale San Diego suburb, they'd be convinced they're right.

Good thing they can't see me.

I draw in a breath, blow it out and look around.

What a place for a bar. The shabby clapboard building has only one light, a sputtering, feeble bulb against the wall. But there are at least fifty cars parked up and down the street and inside, raucous laughter and pulsating music, punctuated by the occasional wild cheer, reverberates like thunder on the still night air.

I draw another impatient breath. Two of the people inside that bar are my partner David, and our skip, John Donaldson. David and I are Bail Enforcement Agents, bounty hunters, and this shouldn't be taking so long.

Maybe Donaldson is giving David a hard time.

That thought brings a smile. My partner is six foot six,

weighs 250 pounds and was a tight end for the Broncos. He's big and looks mean, more than a match for John Donaldson, whose rap sheet showed a skinny, anxious man with thinning hair and wire rim glasses perched atop a bulbous nose—an accountant of all things.

I stretch and yawn, and do a few squats to stretch taut leg muscles, not easy when you're wearing three-inch heels and a short skirt.

Still, there's not much chance he's giving David trouble. Besides the obvious, Donaldson is nothing but a white-collar wannabe who played fast and loose with his employer's pension fund. When they caught up with the idiot, his string of shady business deals landed him in jail on embezzlement charges instead of in the morgue, where that same enraged employer threatened to send him. Fifty thousand dollars and some pricey La Jolla real estate got him released pending trial. He skipped about the same time his wife found out he'd been keeping a mistress. She became instantly cooperative. She wasn't about to lose her house because the creep decided to jump bail.

But the infidelity—that's her problem. We work for the irate bondsman who will be out a cool five hundred thou if we don't get him back in custody tonight.

Which is exactly what we intend to do.

This should be a piece of cake. Donaldson doesn't have a history of violence. Why he ran is still a mystery considering, as it turns out, he didn't run far. We discovered him holed up in Chula Vista, in a South Bay low-rent district, no less, with the same blond bimbo who caused his wife to give him up. We assume he plans to beat it south to Mexico, but for whatever reason, he hasn't yet.

Still, he's been a slippery little bugger. We thought we had him twice before and he managed to elude us.

But not tonight.

Tonight Donaldson decided to take a little excursion to a sports bar all by himself. It's a perfect setup. Once someone recognizes David, the reaction is predictable. And someone will recognize him—ex-football jock, local hero, David attracts attention the way the North Pole attracts a compass. Then it should be a simple matter of getting Donaldson's undivided attention. David will buy him a few drinks to loosen him up, maybe, or invite him to his place to see his Heismann trophy or Super Bowl Rings. Anything to get him outside.

After that, it's a trip downtown, a little paperwork, and five thousand dollars deposited into our account in the morning.

Easy money. Especially for me. Tonight I'm the designated driver.

So what's the holdup?

I roll my shoulders. I want a nice, cool bath. I want out of these clothes.

Come on, David, I repeat like a mantra; let's get this over with.

I can't stand waiting anymore. The smell is getting to me. If I cross to the other side of the parking lot, I can look through the bar's front door and see what's going on. Maybe David needs a little help. A short skirt and high heels may be a better inducement to Donaldson than trophies and big diamond rings. And I'll still be close enough to beat it back to the car if they're on their way out.

Anything is better than cooling my heels in this stupid alley.

I start across. The throbbing bass is shaking the place and grows louder with each step. David must be deaf by now.

But it's not so loud that it drowns out a familiar voice bellowing across the lot. "Hey, Donaldson, where do you think you're going?"

Shit. Something went wrong. I reverse directions and scurry back to the car. I hear the thump of running feet before I actually see two shadowy forms sprinting toward me. No time for pepper spray or the Taser. And no way am I going to let this jerk get away from us a third time. I unclip my .38 from my belt, take a deep breath, and wait for them to get just a little closer before I step out.

The gun has the desired effect.

Donaldson pulls up short, eyes riveted on the gun leveled at his middle. "What is this? What do you want?"

His face is devoid of color and looks different from his mug shot—leaner and meaner. His black eyes are sunk deep into their sockets and flash in the dim light like a cat's.

Those eyes are disconcerting, but I shake it off and put on a bright smile. "Let me give you a hint. You have a court date tomorrow. For some reason, your wife is afraid you might be planning to miss it. Might have something to do with that blonde you've been shacking up with."

David moves up behind him. He slips handcuffs from his pocket and leans his head close. "So, we're your escorts. No need to thank us. It's compliments of your full service bail bondsman."

Donaldson smiles, his mouth cracking in a cold, humorless slit. "You work for Reese? Why didn't you say so? Listen, I've got money. I can double what he's paying you right now." He steps toward me, his hand moving to a pocket in his jacket.

I take a step backward at the same time David grabs for his hand.

"Against the car," David barks. "Spread 'em."

But with amazing quickness, Donaldson ducks under David's restraining arm and is off again across the parking lot.

David groans. "I don't fucking believe this. Anna, start the car. I'll stop this bastard if I have to shoot his ass to do it."

I can't remember the last time anyone got away from David. Once he collars someone, they generally stay collared. This is definitely an annoyance. A sarcastic comment about David letting this guy get away springs to my lips, but when a gunshot explodes behind me, it dies in my throat.

For a moment, I'm frozen in place, hand on the car door. There is no longer the sound of running feet. David has disappeared. I crouch down, work my way around to the front of the car. Where is he? Did he actually fire at Donaldson? Did Donaldson have a gun? Shit, we hadn't gotten a chance to frisk the guy.

The taste of bile burns the back of my throat. Why

isn't David calling out to me? I tighten my grip on the .38 and push to my feet. I know he must be hurt or he'd be yelling.

I'm trying so hard to see what's in front of me that when the attack comes, it's from behind and without warning.

Donaldson is suddenly beside me, wrenching my right arm back. The pain causes my hand to open reflexively and I watch my gun skid across the pavement. Then I'm slammed into the car.

"So, hot shot," he says. "What are you going to do now?"

His breath smells of alcohol and rage. He's knocked the wind out of me and I gasp for air. My right arm feels like it's going to snap. I fight to catch my breath, to keep the fear out of my voice. He's much too strong. "Get off me, Donaldson. You're breaking my arm."

He laughs, torquing my arm even higher. "Where's that partner of yours, huh? Maybe you'll be more cooperative now without him."

I try to straighten up, to take some of the pressure off my arm, but he pushes me back against the car with no effort. He's on something; he must be. I can't control the speed of my words—they tumble out in a rush. "Listen, Donaldson, you're already in trouble with the law. I know David must be hurt. Let me help him. We're not cops. You know you can leave now. Don't make it worse for yourself."

But he's still laughing, the sound so harsh and grating it seems to burn my cheek. "What makes you think I'm in a hurry to leave?"

I'm pinned against the car with his body. His hands begin groping. My stomach muscles constrict. I shove back against him, fighting to gain leverage. "Someone will have heard the shot in the bar. They'll come out."

But he cocks his head in the direction of the bar. "With that racket? I don't think so. Go on, scream."

I do, yelling until my throat hurts. The noise from the bar swallows my cries.

"See? What did I tell you?" He fumbles at the buttons on my blouse. "I think we should get to know each other better, don't you?" He gives up on the buttons and rips it open, spinning me around to face him.

I try to fight him off. I'm five-foot-five inches tall and weigh 125 pounds. He's not much taller or heavier, but he overpowers me as if I were a child. He grabs my hair and yanks my head back. He's got the door open, and he pushes me down onto the backseat. I gouge at his face and neck, drawing blood that looks thick and black in the dark. He acts like he's oblivious to the pain. I'm pinned under him, pitching and bucking against his weight, but I can't shake him off. He's unbuckled his pants, one hand holding me down, the other working at the zipper. I don't have room to kick at him, so in desperation, I reach between his legs and grab and squeeze.

In the darkness, I don't see the blow coming. There's a brief flash of exploding color. Then, nothing.

CHAPTER 2

I DON'T WANT TO WAKE UP. I'M IN A WARM, DARK cocoon, floating, safe.

Still, a blinding light intrudes on the darkness. Someone is forcing my eyes open. I push the hand away. It comes back. From far away I hear my own voice. "Will you shut off that damned light?"

A chuckle. "She's back, Doc."

The voice is familiar. I open my eyes. "David?"

"Right here, sweetheart." A gentle hand finds mine. "How do you feel?"

I try to turn my head; the pain stops me. I reach up to touch my face, feel a huge, painful lump and wince. "Not too good. What happened?"

He doesn't answer. I struggle to focus, struggle to turn my head slowly in the direction of his voice. I know that I should be remembering something—something that triggers a spasm of alarm even through the haze of confusion.

David is seated beside me in a wheelchair, neck bulging out of a brace that looks so tight, it bites into his skin. "That looks comfortable," I say grimly. "Where are we?"

But someone steps between us. He's tall and thin with a disheveled mop of red hair. He's in scrubs, a stethoscope dangling from his neck. He smiles down at me. "You're in County General Hospital, Anna," he says. "My name is Grant Avery. I'm the doctor who has been taking care of you."

"Me? Why?" As soon as I ask that, something dangerous and threatening flashes again, like a foggy image in the back of my mind, and I flinch without knowing why.

David pushes himself closer. "It's going to be all right."

Dr. Avery nods. "David is right. You're both going to be just fine. Do you remember what happened to you?"

My temples throb with dull repetition. I bring up a hand to press away the pain and notice the needle sticking out of the back of it. Bright red blood flows through the tubing. I let the hand drop. "No. Have I been here long?"

"Since before dawn yesterday," the doctor responds.

"Yesterday?" I glance at David. "I've been out since yesterday?"

David's slow, sweet smile doesn't quite reach his eyes when he says, "You went a little crazy in the ambulance. You've been sedated since then."

"The ambulance?" I keep repeating things. I can't stop myself because nothing he tells me makes sense. "What ambulance?"

David looks up at Dr. Avery. "Maybe you should tell her."

"Someone should tell me." I try to make that sound convincing, though I'm beginning to wonder if I want to remember. Whatever happened is obviously not good.

It's Dr. Avery who breaks the silence. "You've been through quite an ordeal, but I want to reassure you that the physical damage inflicted on you will not, in any way, be permanently disabling." He glances at his watch, then back at me. "You were badly beaten. You've got a nasty contusion on your forehead—that's what's causing the headache. It's also why you seem to have lost your memory. But it's what we call retrograde amnesia—short term. You have two black eyes, but no concussion. Your eyes are not damaged." He pauses, again with a glance at his watch.

"You have somewhere else to be?" I ask, irritation spiking with each glance at his watch. I have the distinct impression that there's more and the good doctor is stalling.

He has the grace to flush slightly. "No, of course not. I was just hoping the counselor would be here before I—"

"Counselor?" The fear reasserts itself. David pushes himself up from the wheelchair and moves to my bedside. His hand tightens around the fingers of my left hand, but I push it away. "Why would I need a counselor?"

Dr. Avery peers down at me. I see the hesitation on his face, but it's not his decision whether or not to continue—it's mine.

"Tell me."

"Are you sure? The counselor will be here in a moment or two. You might feel better having a woman here with you. Or we could call someone from your family." A glance at my partner. "David seemed to think you might want to wait on that, but it's really your call."

I look over at David, too, but his expression is so solemn and sad it makes me all the more afraid. "David is right about the family thing," I say quietly. "Now tell me what the hell happened."

I pull my eyes away from David and wait for the doctor to continue.

"You were sexually assaulted, Anna." His voice is matter-of-fact, controlled. Now his eyes never leave my face. "You've suffered considerable trauma to the lower part of your body. Your arms are badly bruised. You've lost a lot of blood from a cut on your neck. The police think whoever did this may have tried to slash your throat. Luckily, he botched the job, but you required a transfusion. Do you want me to go on?"

My fingers are on the bandage at the side of my neck. Someone tried to rape me and cut my throat? How could there be more? I realize Dr. Avery is waiting. Numbly, I nod. "Go on."

He nods once, too, those unblinking eyes holding me captive. "Because there was evidence of penetration, we had to run pregnancy tests. They were negative. However, there are other tests that will take longer to process.

We'll screen for sexually transmitted diseases, hepatitis . . ." A brief hesitation, "HIV."

He runs through the laundry list of horrors in a detached, mechanical way. When his voice drops away, so do his eyes, releasing me from their hold.

There must be a mistake. I sneak a look at David's face. The truth is stamped there in stark relief. "I can't remember it," I whisper. "Maybe that's a good thing."

David and Dr. Avery exchange a look. Then the doctor picks up a chart from the foot of the bed and moves toward the door. "I'll give you two a few minutes," he says.

David watches until the door closes behind him. "Anna," he says softly, "I'm so sorry."

I press the palms of my hands against my eyes, mindful now of why I'm here, but still unable to call up the how. "Tell me what happened."

"Are you sure you're ready?"

Will I ever be? "Yes."

David perches himself carefully on the edge of the bed. He picks up my left hand again and strokes it gently. "I'll tell you what I know."

CHAPTER 3

DAVID'S VOICE IS UNCHARACTERISTICALLY hesitant as he begins. "I screwed up, Anna," he says. "I should have recognized that Donaldson was on something in the bar. He was jumpy and unfocused, but he wasn't drinking. When he found out who I was, he seemed really interested in coming with me. We got outside, and out of the blue, he starts running. At first I thought he must have figured out why I was after him. But he never said anything; he just took off."

His voice drops, waiting, I suppose, for me to give some indication that any of this makes sense. It doesn't. I shake my head and wave a hand at him to go on.

David rubs a hand over his eyes. "I yelled at him to stop. You were at the car. He ran right at you and you stopped him. That's when he found out we were from Reese. He offered us money to let him go. Before we could cuff him, he took off again. The little shit can really run. I got him cornered, though, between two cars. He turned on me, and I swear to God, Anna, he started growling and snarling like a wild dog. I figured this guy is really whacked. He came at me. It was like a blur. He slammed into me, and I lost my balance and went down, hit my knee against a bumper. I hit my head on something, too, I guess, because the next thing I remember, I wake up and it's quiet and I have the worst headache I've ever had in my life."

He stops again and color flushes his face. "Stupid thing to say. A headache seems pretty lame compared to what—"

I hold up a hand, impatient, irritated. "Stop it, David. You were hurt, too. You couldn't help what happened to me. Just tell me what you remember next."

David pushes himself off the bed and starts pacing. "It was so dark in that lot. I figured it had to be after two, because it was quiet and most of the cars were gone. I called out to you, but there was no answer. Just about the time I got my legs back under me, I heard shouting. The bartender and some of the staff found you on their way out. Evidently, they scared Donaldson off. They said they saw a man running away, but he moved too fast for them to make an ID. They called for help."

He's stopped his pacing and is watching me now, waiting for a reaction. Trouble is, I don't know how to react. I can see the bruises, feel the pain and watch the blood flow through the tube attached to the back of my hand. But I don't *remember.* It's as if I'm hearing about something terrible that happened to someone close to me. Revulsion is there, and anger, but it's not personal. At least, not yet.

I do suddenly remember what David said earlier. "This happened twenty-four hours ago. You told me I've been sedated because of something that happened in the ambulance. What did I do?"

The beginnings of a smile tweak the corners of David's mouth before he stops it and his expression grows still and serious again. "You gave the paramedics quite a turn. You were unconscious until those ambulance doors shut and then you went ballistic. You started right in swinging, almost broke the jaw of one of the attendants. I had to help them subdue you. You were really out of it, ranting about wild animals and being bitten. Dr. Avery says it was a reaction to the neck wound and the viciousness of Donaldson's attack, but he didn't want to take the chance that it might happen again. He kept you well sedated until he could bring you out of it gradually. Like he did this morning."

This morning. A wave of weariness washes over me and I close my eyes. I feel David shift at my side and look up to find him bending close, his face a marble effigy of concern. I try to smile but the muscles of my own face are frozen. The best I can do is grimace, which makes the muscles along David's jaw clench even tighter in distress. He grabs my hand again and squeezes.

"Anna, what's wrong? Are you in pain? Should I call the doctor back?"

"Probably." I glance down. "I may need him to set the bones you're breaking in my hand."

He releases the death grip. "Sorry."

I've known my partner a long time and we've found

ourselves in some tough situations, but I've never seen him scared before. It's disconcerting, especially since I know I should be feeling worse than he does.

Why don't I?

Is it just the memory loss? Am I in shock?

I draw a deep breath, hold it, and then blow it out. "David, it's all right. I'm going to be just fine. You've spoken to the police, haven't you? What did they say? Did they catch up with Donaldson?"

He shakes his head and pulls at the neck brace in irritation. "No. Donaldson is still on the loose. But they'll get him, and when they do, he won't be able to deny he attacked you. They got blood and hair samples from the car. Tissue samples from under your fingernails."

I get a flash of a lab technician somewhere opening a box with my name on it and withdrawing sealed envelopes with swabs and scrapings. Proof of what Donaldson did to me. Then I drag myself back to listen as David drones on.

"Seminal fluid, vaginal secretions—" David suddenly seems to realize what he's describing—evidence of a rape—and he stops short. "Anyway," he says after a long moment. "As soon as you can, they'll want your statement."

"And with any luck," a voice from the doorway interjects, "you will be able to give that statement very soon."

Dr. Avery is back in the room. He joins David at my bedside. I notice for the first time the tiny laugh lines radiating from the corners of his eyes and the touches of humor around his mouth as he smiles down at me.

A smile that warms me.

"Your blood work is just about finished, Anna," he says. "If you feel up to it, I see no reason why you can't be released early this evening." He looks at David. "I assume you'll be able to take her home?"

David's eyes widen. "Take her home? It's too soon. She hasn't spoken to a counselor. And didn't you say she lost a lot of blood? She can't be strong enough yet."

The doctor ignores David and crosses to the other side of the bed where he begins the process of unhooking the various tubes feeding into my veins. There are two, one with a clear liquid attached to my arm, and the second, the blood line on the back of my hand. There's a brief stinging sensation as he withdraws that needle and presses a compress against the wound, gesturing for me to hold it in place.

I move my fingers over his and he lets go.

"Anna should be feeling stronger now," he says, his competent, sure fingers at my wrist. His eyes study the stainless steel Rolex on his own as he takes my pulse. "You are, aren't you?"

I am. The realization hits with an unpredictable consequence. I find myself smiling—a real smile—at the doctor. He smiles back and nods.

But David is obviously not convinced. "It's too soon," he insists again. "She doesn't have her memory back yet. What if everything that Donaldson did to her comes back when she's alone? That can't be good."

Dr. Avery seems to consider his words. "You may be right," he says. "Anna, how do you feel about being alone? If you're concerned, maybe you could stay with family for a few days?"

not even a consideration, though I
"No. My folks left yesterday for Europe.
can take care of myself."

ot yet, you can't," David says.

His persistence is beginning to grate. "David, if Dr. Avery thinks I'm all right on my own, what's the problem?"

"I just don't like it. Max is gone—"

The mention of my boyfriend's name brings me up short. I haven't thought of Max since the attack. I'm not ready to think about him now.

I look over at Dr. Avery. "There may be someone else," I say. "I have a good friend."

David glares at me. He knows who I'm thinking of. "Not Michael."

"Why not?"

He's looking at me as if I'm crazy for even considering it. But I have my reasons for thinking of Michael, reasons I'm going to share with David—when we're alone. Right now, I shake my head.

"David, who else is there? If you don't want me to be alone, it's got to be Michael."

"No," he insists. "It doesn't have to be Michael. You could stay with me."

I actually laugh out loud. "Oh. That's a good idea. Your girlfriend will be thrilled. Gloria hates me already. If I stay with you, you'll have to taste my food and stay up all night to be sure she doesn't stab me in my sleep."

His expression shifts from concern to indignation. "Gloria does not hate you. Why do you say things like that?"

But before I can reply, Dr. Avery has stepped between

us, a frown tugging at the corners of his mouth. "I didn't mean to start something here," he says to David with a spark of impatience. "It's really up to Anna whether she wants to be alone or not. And if she doesn't, I think she's perfectly capable of choosing who she'd be most comfortable with."

I look at Dr. Avery, a little surprised at the way he's sticking up for me. But I also see how this is affecting David. Dr. Avery's strident tone causes David to bristle. I can see by the set of his jaw and the little vein starting to pulse in his forehead that's he's close to telling Dr. Avery exactly what he can do with his opinions.

I raise myself up off the pillow. "Okay, guys, can we take a step back here?"

The length of a heartbeat passes before the two men break eye contact and swivel toward me.

"David, I appreciate your concern. I really do. But Gloria will not want me in your house—" He raises a hand to protest, but I know what he's going to say and I cut him off. "It doesn't matter the reason. She resents the fact that I'm in your life at all. She thinks you're in the bounty hunting business because of me instead of the other way around."

Dr. Avery looks from one of us to the other. "How *did* the two of you get together?"

David ignores the question. In fact, he's trying hard to ignore Dr. Avery, so I answer. "David didn't like the prospects open to retired ex-football players. Selling used cars or becoming a sports newscaster. I didn't like teaching. We answered the same ad from a bail bondsman looking for some help doing skip tracing. Turns out, David and I made a good team and before long, we had our own business."

David makes a grunting sound. "None of which has anything to do with where you should go when you get out of here."

"But it has everything to do with Gloria hating me. She thinks it's my fault you're not living with her in L.A."

Dr. Avery casts an inquisitive glance toward David. "L.A.?"

Once again, David makes it a point to ignore Dr. Avery's question. Once again, I answer.

"Gloria is a big-time model. You know those Victoria's Secret commercials on TV? Then you know Gloria."

He looks impressed. Most men do. It's very irritating.

"So. Right." It comes out a little shriller than I intend. I draw in a breath, blow it out. "Anyway, Michael has been my best friend since grade school. He can take care of me better than anyone."

David opens his mouth, but Dr. Avery cuts in first. "It's settled then. Anna, I want you to try standing up now. I'll send a nurse in to help you shower. We'll keep you here long enough to make sure you can get around, and then you can call your friend."

A virulent combination of anger, revulsion and disbelief flashes across David's face. "I don't believe this."

His tone is deceptively quiet. It's a bad sign. "Thank you, Dr. Avery," I say, waving him out of the room. "Let me just talk to David a minute before you send in that nurse."

David's fury emanates from him like shock waves.

Fortunately, Dr. Avery seems to sense it and beats a hasty retreat.

When the door has closed behind him, I push myself to the edge of the bed. "Want to help me up?"

My voice snaps David's attention from Dr. Avery to me. The expression drops from his face like a mask to be replaced by one just as unsettling. He gives me a bleak, tight-lipped smile. "I'm sorry, Anna," he says. "I just don't see what Michael could do for you that I can't. And I resent like hell that bastard Avery taking a position on something that's none of his business. He doesn't know you. Or Michael."

As he talks, David is helping me off the bed. Once I'm standing, I let his comments go while I take inventory. I feel surprisingly strong. I'm a little sore but my legs hold and I'm able to let go of David's steadying arm.

David frowns. "You sure you're okay?"

I take the two steps over to a sink against the wall of my room and look into the mirror.

That's when it starts coming back.

CHAPTER 4

DONALDSON IS ON TOP OF ME, HOLDING MY arms at my side. *Are you awake? I want you awake. It's no fun otherwise.*

I hear the voice from inside my head. I think it's a trick, that I'm dreaming or still unconscious.

But the voice comes again.

Come on, Anna. I know you can hear me. We've had an unintentional exchange of bodily fluids. My bad. But you won't have to endure this long. Open your eyes. Look at me.

I don't want to. I try to keep them closed, actually squeeze them tight with all my strength, but my eyes open anyway. I turn my head to avoid looking at Donaldson, but steel fingers take my chin and force my face upward.

That's a good girl. No, don't try to fight. You can't fight me. Just look into my eyes. Do you like what you see?

Yellow eyes, slit like a cat's, stare down.

And something else. A snarling mouth with tiny, pointed teeth.

I start to scream, struggle again to break free.

Donaldson just laughs. His hands are everywhere—on my breasts, between my legs, tearing open the collar of my blouse, exposing my neck.

I do the only thing I can. I bite him again and again, feel the skin on his cheek and neck tear, taste the copper of his blood in my mouth.

It doesn't seem to faze him. He bunches up my skirt, opens his pants and pushes against me. His mouth is hot on my neck, his teeth pinch and tear and finally break through.

Everything changes.

His hardness electrifies me. I feel a thrill of arousal.

No.

I don't want this.

"Yes, you do," he answers as if I've spoken it aloud.

Then he's inside me, filling me, driving me to the brink.

A moan escapes my lips. I arch up to meet him, using my legs around his waist to lock him to me, using my hands to clasp his head tight against my neck. I lap and suck hungrily at the blood dripping from his cheek. My body vibrates with liquid fire.

I don't want it to stop. Any of it. I can't get enough.

CHAPTER 5

"ANNA?"

David's voice from far away.

"Anna? What's wrong? You're white as a sheet."

His words are distorted, as if he's speaking underwater. His hand is on my shoulder, guiding me back to the bed.

"I knew it was too soon for you to be up. That damned Avery. What kind of sadistic quack is he? I'm going to get a new doctor in here to see you right now."

His diatribe continues well past the minute it takes me to drag myself back from the . . . what? Nightmare? Vision?

Memory?

It seemed very real. And it strengthened one terrible, nagging suspicion growing in the back of my mind. Was it really rape? And if it was, why am I not feeling what I should be?

What the hell happened in that car?

I find myself at the edge of the bed, looking up at David. Confusion and concern shadow his features. He's trying to urge me to lie back down. I don't want to. I shake off his hand, gently.

"It's all right." God, how many times have I said that today? "I guess I got up too quickly. I felt a little faint, that's all." His expression shifts to disbelief. "Please, David, I need to get out of here. I'll be fine with Michael."

"Michael again?" A muscle flicks angrily at his jaw. "Jesus, Anna, how can he help you through this better than I? I don't care how long you've known him. I was with you when it happened. I feel responsible. You're my partner." His voice drops in despair. "I should have been watching your back, not out cold in some damned parking lot. This is my fault."

There it is. Guilt. He thinks he could have prevented what happened. "I don't blame you for what happened, David. We've been in dangerous situations before. We're in a dangerous business. I accepted the risk when I took the job. We were both hurt last night, not just me. And we're both going to recover."

"Maybe," he says softly. "But my injuries are just physical. What he did to you is more than that. He *violated* you, for god's sake. Can you ever really recover from something like that?"

Something like what? I'm sick with the notion that I might have been more of a willing participant than a victim. Not something I can say out loud.

When I don't respond, David continues. "Let me at

least try to make it up to you. Stay with me. Or I'll come stay at your house. No Gloria to give us grief."

He's changing tactics. His tone is light, teasing. Maybe it's time to ease his mind. I've taken a seat at the edge of the bed and I pat the place next to me. He sinks down, carefully, the neck brace restricting his movements. "You don't think Michael is the right person to see me through this and I know why. It has nothing to do with Michael and everything to do with you. You're feeling guilty."

He opens his mouth to object, but I cut him off with a wave of my hand. "I'm going to tell you a secret about Michael. When we were in college, some frat boys waited for him outside a bar. They beat the crap out of him and left him for dead for no other reason than he was gay. I took care of him. He does understand about violation. I think better than you. You've always been big and intimidating. I doubt anyone ever tried jumping you, did they?"

His face colors slightly.

"Well," I add, "except for Donaldson, of course. And we both agree that was a fluke. You tripped or something, right?"

He doesn't agree or disagree, but he doesn't argue with me, either.

I take that as a good sign. "And as for Dr. Avery, I'm getting out of here today. You don't need to go ruffle any feathers by demanding I have a new doctor. Besides, I like him. He's cute."

It works. David actually smiles a real smile. "God," he says. "You're a piece of work."

I put my arms around him and hug, carefully, mindful of the brace. "When is this thing coming off?" I ask him, drumming gentle fingers against the stiff collar.

He responds by pulling at it, the Velcro fastenings releasing with a ripping sound as he tugs. "Now." He tosses it away and works his neck, stretching his head from side to side and forward and back. "Much better."

I raise an eyebrow. "Should you have done that?"

"Hey, you forget. I spent ten years in the NFL. I've been banged up much worse than this."

Having a regular conversation with David feels good. No angst and recrimination, just talk. I push myself up. "Okay, I'm going to try this standing and walking thing again. More slowly, this time. Will you go fetch that nurse?"

I'M STANDING UNDER A STREAM OF HOT WATER, back against the shower wall, letting the water wash over and around me. A nurse waits outside the bathroom door, on the off chance that I should need help. But I know I won't. My legs are no longer shaky, and my head is clear. I know it's my imagination, but even the bruises on my face seem less pronounced, and the laceration at my forehead is closing. Only the wound at my neck throbs and burns as the water plays over it.

The wound at my neck.

I close my eyes and turn my face to the wall. I told David that I would call Michael after my shower and that he should go on home and let Gloria take care of him for a few days. That I would be in touch soon.

But even as I said it, I knew I wouldn't make that call. I need to be alone for a while. I need to sort through the disturbing images that keep breaking through my subconscious and asserting themselves into my thoughts.

Donaldson did something to my body in the backseat of that car. Something base and animalistic that I responded to.

I responded to it.

Could I have been drugged? That doesn't make sense. He didn't force me to drink anything. He didn't jam a pill down my throat or stick a needle in my arm. He just—

Just what?

What the hell did he do?

DR. AVERY PAYS ME ONE LAST VISIT BEFORE I LEAVE the hospital. He has my discharge papers in his hand, but he looks cautiously around the room before coming in.

"Your friend is gone?"

I nod. "Sorry about David. He's very protective."

"Understandably." Dr. Avery approaches. "You are in an unusual line of work."

"Especially for a woman, right, Doctor?"

He smiles in a sheepish way that confirms I'd guessed what he was thinking.

"It's okay. I get that all the time." Particularly from my family.

I hold out a hand. "Those for me?"

He hands me the clipboard and a pen and points to

the place I should sign. "Have you made arrangements to be picked up?"

I nod without hesitation. I don't want him to know my plans any more than I want David to know. I have only one small problem. Clothes. I can't very well walk out of here in this air-conditioned hospital gown.

"I don't suppose the gift shop sells anything I could wear home, does it?" I ask, handing the signed forms back to him. "Michael doesn't have a key to my house. I'd hate for him to have to come here and pick it up, drive all the way to the beach for my clothes and then back to the hospital again. I'm kind of anxious to get home."

He doesn't even hesitate a second. "I think I can find a pair of scrubs you can borrow. Will that do?"

"Perfectly."

He starts to say something else, but the door opens again. This time Gloria sweeps into the room, David trailing behind. And I mean that literally. Gloria enters a room like the Queen Mother—imperiously—and everyone else gets sucked along in her wake.

Avery almost swoons. His mouth drops open in a stupid, awestruck sort of way.

"Hello, Gloria," I say without the least bit of inflection. "This is Dr. Avery."

He doesn't say anything, but his mouth does snap shut. And Gloria receives his silent tribulation as she always does, with little regard and great condescension.

She looks wonderful. She has that model figure, all tits and ass and long, long legs. She's wearing a pair of designer sweats—small white crop-top and low slung, curve-hugging bottoms. Her dark hair is swept up in a knot, as if she just came from an exercise class. Her face is devoid of makeup, but that flawless complexion and those huge dark eyes don't need any enhancement. She's beautiful.

And she bloody well knows it.

She's pursing full, pink-tinted lips in my direction. "Anna, David told me what happened. Are you all right?"

I wish there was just the teeniest little note of concern in that voice, but there isn't. It's purely a rhetorical question asked for David's benefit, I'm sure.

"Yes, Gloria. I'm fine. Thanks for asking."

"Good. Glad to hear it." She tilts her head and squints at me. "You don't look half as bad as I expected. Well—except for the hair, of course."

David shoots her a look, but my hands go instinctively to my head. I forgot I'd only towel-dried my hair after my shower. Shit.

Gloria puts a possessive hand on David's arm. "Well, we only stopped by to let you know that David and I are leaving. I know he said you have a friend coming to take care of you, but remember you can call us if you need anything."

The offer hangs in the air while we eye each other. Right.

She makes a move toward the door, but David hangs back a minute. He's frowning at me. "I still don't like this. You sure you're going to be okay?"

I smile. "Yes. Michael will be here any minute." The lie comes easily.

"Call me tonight, okay?"

I nod, again catching Gloria's eye. I know full well if I call tonight, Gloria will answer the phone and I'll be a wrong number.

David comes closer, bends, gives me a kiss on the cheek. "We're going to L.A. for a few days. We leave tomorrow morning. But you have my cell phone number. Call me if you need anything. I'm only a twenty minute commuter flight away."

I nod again and they're gone. The news that David's leaving for L.A. is a relief. It will give me a few days to sort out what's happened on my own. No danger of an unexpected visit. I look toward the doctor.

He's still watching the door Gloria disappeared through, as though hoping to conjure her back again.

"Dr. Avery?"

He gives himself a shake, licks his lips and turns back to me. He has a dazed, questioning look in his eye. He's completely forgotten me, why he's here, and what he's supposed to be doing.

Gloria has that effect on people. Or more specifically, Gloria has that effect on men.

Maybe she's a witch. A real witch, not just the bitchy cousin.

"The scrubs?" I remind him gently. "You were going to get me something to wear."

His eyes clear and he jerks upright. "Of course. I'll be right back." He clutches the clipboard to his chest and rushes out, hoping, no doubt, to snatch one last glimpse of the goddess.

Great.

I open the closet door. My purse is on the floor and I

snatch it up and head back into the bathroom. There's a comb inside and I go to work on hair tangled from the shower. No wonder Dr. Avery swooned when Gloria showed up. I look like the "before" picture in a bad hair ad. I keep my hair short for convenience, but it does need to be combed once in a while, and right now it stands up in peaks like a fright-show wig. Gloria must have had to really restrain herself from bursting into laughter when she saw me.

I peer at my reflection more closely. It's also no wonder Gloria didn't think I looked that bad. Damned, if those black eyes don't seem less pronounced. And the wound on my forehead appears to be closing itself even as I watch.

What is this?

I hear the outside door open. "Dr. Avery," I call. "Look at this—"

But when I step into the room, he isn't there. On the bed a pair of hospital-green scrubs have been left in a neat, folded pile.

Guess I've seen the last of Dr. Avery.

CHAPTER 6

I LIVE ON ISTHMUS COURT IN MISSION BEACH, on a street so narrow, there's no vehicle access. So I direct the cab driver to let me out on busy Mission Blvd. I walk the block to my home, dodging the summer surge of pedestrians that use my street as a beach access, drawn like lemmings to the sea. It's often a nuisance, the noise and pollution, but I wouldn't live anywhere else.

My grandparents bought this place in the fifties, when charming, red shake bungalows were the norm. Now, mine is the only original cottage on the block, dwarfed by pretentious two- and three-story monstrosities that rise out of the ground like monuments to greed. It's a constant irritation what developers and new money are doing to the neighborhood.

I'm only glad my grandmother didn't see it. She gave the cottage to me when she moved to Florida fifteen years ago. She died unexpectedly soon after, and I've lived here ever since—through college, through various forays into "real jobs" approved by my folks. Her gift is what gave me the security I needed to leave a teaching job I hated and, eventually, to discover something that I loved.

I don't think my parents have ever forgiven her for that.

I pick up the newspapers lying on the porch and the dozen or so flyers from real estate agents inquiring as to whether I'd consider selling. They all assure me they have instant buyers, as I'm sure they do. But the smell of the ocean right outside my door and the brilliance of the sun bouncing off the water remind me of why I'd never leave—for any amount of money.

I open the door and breathe deeply, loving the familiar fragrance of cedar paneling mingled with the lodge scent of a real wood burning fireplace and the hint of my grandfather's cigars. It's comforting and welcoming and gives me a sense of belonging. My roots are here in this cottage.

I pick up the phone to check for messages. There are three. My mother, apologizing for the fight we had two nights ago. Jerry Reese, the bail bondsman David and I work for, apologizing for not coming to the hospital to see us and wondering, incidentally, when we'd be available again for work. No mention of Donaldson or what happened to me. Curious. And the third from Max, my boyfriend, apologizing for not checking in sooner, but this was the first chance he's had in days and he's sorry he missed me.

Three messages, three apologies. I delete them all. I'll talk to my mother when they return from vacation. Jerry can wait until David comes back from L.A. I'm not about to go after Donaldson again on my own. And Max—he's DEA, in a deep undercover operation. There's no way I can call him back and there's no telling when I'll hear from him again. The relief I feel at that is no surprise.

I cross into the kitchen, tossing the newspapers on the table. My stomach is rumbling. No wonder. It's almost three o'clock, and I can't remember the last time I ate. I open the refrigerator and peer inside. There's plenty of food—luncheon meats, salad stuff, yogurt.

And the leftover lasagna from my favorite Italian place.

My salivary glands are working overtime.

I pull the covered dish out of the refrigerator and take it to the microwave. I work the corners of the cardboard take-out box loose and hold it up to savor the sweet aroma of meat sauce laced with garlic.

A wave of nausea hits, so overpowering that the container slips from my hand. The lasagna splatters across the counter in a greasy smear.

Shit.

I grab for a sponge and start mopping up, but the smell assaults me again. I can barely stand to scrape the mess into the garbage disposal but the thought of leaving it is even worse. I gag and choke, but finally the last of it whirls down the drain and I draw a cautious breath.

What the hell was that? I've never known lasagna to go bad.

I'm still hungry, so it's back to the refrigerator. But nothing else appeals. I close the door and think. What do I want to eat?

A steak. My second favorite food in all the world.

I do an abrupt about face, snatch up a newspaper and my purse, and head out the back door. There's a dive right down the street that serves the very best steaks in town.

I'VE TAKEN A SEAT ON THE PATIO FACING THE boardwalk. One of the things I like most about living on the beach is the constant, ever changing, ever surprising, variety of people drawn to the water. It's the greatest show on earth. The ocean is truly the great leveler. It strips inhibitions, frees the psyche. All bare toes look the same covered with beach sand.

It's why I can sit here in baggy scrubs and bad hair and not draw the least bit of attention.

And, most importantly, it's why Jorge, my server, doesn't look askance at my garb or at my face as I place my order.

It also confirms my suspicion that my metabolism must be much better than I expected. I know I'm in good shape; I exercise and watch my diet. Still, I'm healing so quickly, there's hardly a bruise or scratch left.

How can that be?

Right now, I don't care. I'm hungry.

But there's something else nagging at me. Mentally, I feel good—really good. I know that's not logical or reasonable. Maybe David is right. I am in shock. I should ask someone. But Dr. Avery never mentioned that tardy counselor again, nor did he leave me her name or number with my discharge papers.

Another peculiar thing.

Jorge is back with my glass of wine and the promise that my steak would be forthcoming. It shouldn't take long. After all, I ordered only steak—no salad, no potatoes or veggies. I feel the need for protein, pure and simple. His acceptance of my order as nothing out of the ordinary is another confirmation of the wonders of beach life. No raised eyebrow, no frown of confusion to mar that wonderful, dusky-hued Latin face.

I think I love him.

I take a sip of wine, sigh, and sit back. The newspaper is at my elbow and I open it, scanning the headlines, wondering what I've missed in the last twenty-four hours. Not much, it seems. I page through the sections one by one. I'm almost through Section C, local news, when a small article at the bottom of page 8 catches my eye. It's about Donaldson and my heart stops. I'm afraid it's going to be about the attack and that my name will be mentioned. I know the rape laws prohibit that, but it takes me a minute to swallow that fear and start reading.

The article turns out to be very different than I expect.

Donaldson is now a fugitive wanted for not only the suspected embezzlement, but sexual battery and murder.

Murder?

I read on. According to the article, Donaldson evidently returned to the apartment in Chula Vista where he killed the woman he had been staying with. She was found with her throat cut. She had been beaten, sexually molested, then washed and left drained and lifeless in the bathtub. It is presumed Donaldson has taken her car and headed to Mexico. A description of the car and license plate number follow, along with a warning to the public that he is considered armed and dangerous and should not be approached.

I lay the paper down and take another sip of wine.

Did he attack his girlfriend before or after he attacked me? An icy finger touches my spine. What did Dr. Avery say? It looked like he tried to cut my throat. I could very well be dead, too.

And yet—

There's nothing in the article at all about what happened to me outside that bar. In fact, it suddenly dawns on me that I haven't been contacted by the police about it, either. Bail enforcement agents are not beloved by most cops, but I was the victim of a crime. I should at least be interviewed. And then there's the matter of my car. It must be in an impound lot somewhere, and once it's been processed for evidence, it should be returned to me.

Why didn't I have a message from the police asking me to get in touch? Did David take care of all that and forget to tell me? Or did he and Dr. Avery convince the cops there was nothing I could contribute—except the physical evidence they collected, of course—until my memory returns?

At least one thing is cleared up—why Jerry didn't mention Donaldson when he called. Because of the new crimes lodged against Donaldson, the court will already have revoked his bail. Jerry would no longer be liable for the bond. Donaldson will be heading straight for jail.

Once he's caught. The longer he's in Mexico, though, the less likely that is.

Jorge appears with my steak, and I dig right in. The succulent meat is tender and bloody—not usually the way I like it. I'm more of a medium well gal. But today, rare is the ticket and it's great. Must have to do with losing so much blood.

I sigh contentedly and chew, letting my thoughts wander to more mundane things as I eat. Laundry to be done, shopping, bills to be paid. I make a mental list of what to do in what order, finish the steak, soaking up all the juices with a slice of bread, wipe at my lips with my napkin and motion to Jorge to bring the check.

I realize as I offer him my credit card that it's been a good twenty minutes and I haven't once thought about what happened in that parking lot. This ambivalence isn't natural and while part of me is grateful that I'm not falling apart, a saner voice of reason knows that something is definitely wrong.

I just can't figure out what it is.

I leave the restaurant and stroll back along the boardwalk to my street. It's six o'clock and the sun is just now burning through. There's something about the quality of sunshine on the beach that's different than anywhere else. Reds and blues and greens are more vivid, which explains why so many beach houses are painted in shades of the rainbow. The clean, clear colors reflect that glorious sunshine and make you happy just to look at them.

I'm feeling that happiness now, basking in it, letting

the warmth of the dry summer sun soak deep into my bones. This is the way it's supposed to be in July. Maybe we've finally broken out of that damned—

But something else gets broken, too. My pleasant reverie. I'm almost home and there's someone leaning against the front gate. He's dressed in ragged cutoffs and a tank top, but that mop of red hair is unmistakable even from a distance.

Dr. Avery is making a house call.

CHAPTER 7

H E PUSHES OFF FROM THE GATE WHEN HE SEES me and joins me at the boardwalk. "I love your place," he says enthusiastically.

He's grinning and looking around, which gives me a chance to give him the once over. The last time I saw him he was in doctor garb, covered from head to toe. Now, however, in this outfit, I'm treated to a display of muscular arms, powerful shoulders, and long, sturdy legs all tanned bronze. It takes me a minute to work my gaze from this tall, unexpectedly athletic form back up to his face. He's wearing black aviator Ray-Bans that shield his eyes, but his mouth reflects unabashed humor as he watches me check him out.

I keep my expression studiously neutral as I meet his gaze. "Did you come for the scrubs?" I ask. "I would have returned them to you, you know. You didn't have to make the trip."

"Nope, not the scrubs." He grins a little wider and dangles a set of car keys in front of my face.

Car keys that look very familiar. "Are those mine?"

"Yep. Thought you might need your car. I made arrangements to get it back for you." A brief pause. "I also took the liberty of having it detailed. It was, well, a little messy inside."

I take the keys from his outstretched hand and look at him with upturned eyebrows. "How did you manage to get my car? I can't imagine the police would just release it to you."

He shrugs. "I have friends in high places." He looks over my shoulder. "Speaking of which, where's your friend Michael? I thought he was bringing you home."

I hesitate. What explanation can I give for being alone?

But he doesn't give me the chance to come up with anything. He jumps right in, giving me a conspiratorial wink. "I suspected you hadn't called him."

His smugness is annoying.

"Oh? How do you know I didn't call him? He could be inside, right now, fixing me dinner."

Those feather-like laugh lines I noticed in the hospital crinkle around the Ray-Bans. "Is he?"

Well, no. But I'm not telling Dr. Avery that. And how the hell does he know I didn't call Michael, anyway?

"I didn't think so," he responds. "Calling that cab to pick you up gave it away."

My jaw sags a little. Had I spoken out loud?

"No," he answers.

That's it. This is getting creepy. "Okay." I put steel in

my voice. "Are you psychic? Is this some kind of trick?"

He puts a hand on my elbow and steers me toward my gate. "Invite me inside," he says. "And I'll answer all your questions."

I pull away. "I don't think so." I don't invite strange men into my home, and this guy is even stranger than most. I have no intention of being alone with him, doctor or no.

Dr. Avery removes his sunglasses. His eyes lock me in their gaze. "I won't hurt you, Anna," he says softly. "In fact, I can help you. You have a lot of questions about what happened to you with Donaldson. I have the answers."

His voice, velvet edged and insistent, sends a ripple of tranquil acceptance through me. I know with absolute certainty that he won't hurt me. Unhesitatingly, I lead the way to the door and unlock it, holding it open for him to pass through. "Welcome to my home."

As Dr. Avery takes a seat on the couch, he grins up at me and says again, "I really do love your home. I mean it, this is a great place."

But I'm not going to be sidetracked. Now that we're inside, that unshakeable confidence I felt just a moment before melts away. I perch myself on the edge of an overstuffed chair facing him. "Now what do you have to tell me about Donaldson?"

As soon as I say it, a primitive warning resonates in my brain. What could he possibly know about Donaldson? Unless he's gotten more of those tests back and—

"No, no, it's nothing medical."

He's done it again. I launch myself up and at him, seething with mounting rage. "Okay, that's it. How are you doing that? It's not funny, it's not clever, and it's really pissing me off."

My outburst doesn't faze him. He crosses one tanned leg over the other and looks right at me.

Try it yourself.

The voice comes out of nowhere. Or rather, it comes from *inside* my head.

See? The voice continues. *Now try saying something to me.*

"What the hell do you mean?"

No. Dr. Avery's brow wrinkles slightly, as though he's concentrating harder. *Don't answer with your voice. Use your mind.*

Are you nuts?

He beams. *Now that wasn't hard, was it?*

I sink back into the armchair, suddenly woozy with surprise and dread. Did I really do that? Project my thoughts to him?

Of course you did, Dr. Avery responds, his face lit up like a child's at Christmas. There's pride and delight and wonder all mingled together. *You are a quick study. I knew it the moment I saw you at the hospital.*

Saw what at the hospital?

I catch him before he can respond in that eerie telepathic way. I hold up a hand and insist grimly, "No. Talk to me. The normal way. This is creeping me out."

A shadow of disappointment replaces the glow on his face. "I thought you'd be at least a little pleased to know how well you're progressing. Most don't come this far this fast."

"Most what?"

He gives me a sideways glance. "Come on. You must know what you're becoming."

The hair on the back of my neck is rising, along with goose bumps the size of marshmallows on my arms. "What I'm becoming?"

He thinks, *You're beginning to sound like a parrot.*

My god, how do I know that?

Out loud, he's saying, "I knew you'd have questions about Donaldson, but I thought they'd be along the 'what can I expect and how do I handle it' line."

"Handle what?"

It seems to finally dawn on Avery that we're not on the same page. Maybe he's not as good at the mind reading thing as he thinks.

Oh, but I am usually, comes the immediate reply. *I don't understand.*

He doesn't understand?

I'm on my feet again, pacing in front of him like a mad woman. "Stop doing that. Don't insinuate yourself into my head. Listen to me. What are you? What am I 'becoming'? What does this have to do with Donaldson? God, I feel like I'm going crazy here."

He hesitates just a second, pursing his lips at me. Then he's on his feet, too. He takes my hand and leads me over to a mirror on the wall beside the door. "Look at me, Anna."

Half afraid, I nevertheless raise my eyes to the glass.

I'm aware of the touch of his hand, feel the nearness of his body next to mine. But he casts no reflection. None. And my own image is hazy and indistinct, fading more even as I watch.

I jump back, heart pounding so hard in my chest, I'm afraid it will burst. "This can't be happening."

Why do you doubt it?

"Stop it." Shock quickly gives way to rage. I fling open the front door. "Get out. I don't want you in my house any longer."

But he doesn't move. He looks at me with sad, compassion-filled eyes. "I can't do that, Anna. You need me. And truth be told, I need you, too. There's something you must do before you join the family."

Family? I'm afraid to think what family that would be.

"The only family you have," Avery answers without prompting. "Now that you are vampire."

CHAPTER 8

V AMPIRE?
    The word hangs in the air between us, black and ominous as a storm cloud. We stare at each other, not moving. I can scarcely breathe. Avery reaches past me and closes the front door. The simple action breaks the impasse and snaps me back. But the rage is gone.

"What are you talking about?"

He gestures to the living room. "Do you want to sit down?"

At least he's talking and not performing that stupid mind trick. I nod and follow him to the couch. We take seats at opposite ends, putting as much distance as possible between us. I push myself to the edge, the urge to flee strong. "Tell me."

"Where do you want me to start?"

I press my hands to my head. "At the beginning, I guess. With Donaldson."

"Do you remember any of it?" But he scans my face and answers on his own. "You do. The images are coming back. The feelings. It's frightening you because you realize you were a participant, not a victim. That's all right. It's natural."

"Natural?" The word explodes out of me. "There is nothing natural about this. I was fighting Donaldson and suddenly I wasn't. God, I actually responded to him—or rather my body did. I had no control. I tasted his blood and—"

The mental picture of Donaldson on top of me, the memory of the taste of his blood in my mouth, of the way I lapped at it and craved it and couldn't get enough, puts a stop to my diatribe. "That's it, isn't it?" I seek affirmation in Dr. Avery's face and find it. "I drank his blood, and he drank mine. God, I thought that was an old wives' tale."

The absurdity of what I just said stops me. I actually laugh, hysteria so close I taste it like something bitter in the back of my throat. "Did you hear that? I'm telling you that I believe I am becoming a vampire because I drank Donaldson's blood. And you, a medical doctor, are sitting here listening to this as if you believe it, too. We must both be crazy. There are no vampires. There are no ghosts, or witches, or fairies, or werewolves. I'm having a really strange dream, and I'm going to wake up now and be normal and none of this will have happened, and you are going to be gone."

The mounting delirium in my voice makes Dr. Avery move a little closer to me on the couch. He doesn't touch me, or reach out, he just sits quietly and waits for me to run out of breath and energy before he says, "It's a lot to accept, I know. But you should consider yourself lucky. Donaldson didn't set out to turn you. He meant to kill you, just the way he did that unfortunate woman who took him in. But two things happened that prevented it. He was interrupted by the men in the bar before he could drain you, and you drank of his blood. There is nothing you could have done to prevent what happened, just as there is nothing you can do to change it. You must accept what you are becoming. I am here to help you."

Whether it's another mind trick or just a good bed-side manner, the resonance and timbre of his voice calms me. "You're here to help me? And how will you do that? Are you a vampire, too? Is there a handbook I have to study? A class in bloodsucking I'm required to attend?"

He smiles and shakes his head. "Let's see, to answer your questions in order. Yes, I'm here to help. I'll do whatever I can to ease your transition. Yes, I'm a vampire, too. And no, there is no handbook and no class. It's strictly on-the-job training, so to speak."

"You can make jokes? What the hell are you?"

"Technically, I'm a Night Watcher."

"A what?"

"A Night Watcher." Avery pushes himself off the couch. "Would you like some water?"

My head is spinning. "No, I don't want any water." I nod as he gestures toward the kitchen. "Yeah, sure. Go for it. There's bottled water in the fridge. No, wait. I thought vampires only drank blood. You drink water?"

"That's good," he says, moving toward the kitchen.

"You are starting to ask the right questions."

The right questions? There's nothing right about this whole situation.

I wait for Avery to chime in. The voice doesn't come. Maybe he's finally conceding to my wish to stay the hell out of my head.

"I'll do whatever it takes to make you comfortable."

Or not.

He's back in the living room, water bottle in hand. "Now, what were we talking about?"

I give up. But I won't play his game. "You were about to tell me what this 'night watching' thing is all about," I say in a loud, clear voice.

He draws on the bottle and sits back down on the couch facing me. "A long time ago, before there were policemen or armies to defend a town, guardians would walk the streets at night with swords and lanterns. They would call out the passing hours and the 'all is well' signal. They were called Night Watchers."

"So this is what you do? Walk the street at night calling 'all is well'? And if that is your job, where the hell were you when Donaldson was attacking me? All was certainly not well then, was it?"

He shakes his head, irritation twisting the corners of his mouth. "I don't mean to say that I literally walk the streets at night. I was trying to give you a point of reference."

I'm glad he's getting pissed off, since he's certainly having that effect on me. "Okay, I get your point of reference. But since we happen to be living in the twenty-first century, it means nothing to me. You want to explain in normal terms exactly what you do?"

The cloud passes from his face. "I am one of a contingent of vampires who watches for signs of activity in a community and intervenes when necessary to preserve the balance between the living and the undead."

The undead? That one phrase makes the rest of his pedantic recitation fade from my mind quicker than a bunny gets fucked. "The undead?" I hear myself screeching. "That's what I am? Undead?"

"Well, technically, yes."

Oh my God. I'm on my feet again, unable to control the violent tremors that pass through my body. My heart is beating like a drum—wait a minute.

My heart.

I press a hand to my chest. Yes, it's beating. Faster than it should, but it's beating. I look up to find Avery watching with an amused grin on his face.

"Yes," he says. "You have a heartbeat. And you will continue to do so unless you give yourself a heart attack with these violent outbursts."

I sink back down on the couch. "I don't understand any of this. How can I be 'undead' and have a heartbeat?"

"There's a long, dry, technical explanation for that," Avery says with a sigh. "Has to do with something called *etheric revenant* or the way a dead human body is stabilized. I can recommend a book for you by John Michael Greer if you want technical information, though he gave the book the unfortunate title, *Monsters*."

Unfortunate?

He waves a hand. "The important thing for you to

know is that you must care for your physical body as you always have. You work it out, you nourish it. It's just the type of nourishment that will change."

Here it comes. "You mean I have to drink blood."

"You need fresh, etheric energy, yes."

"I don't think I can accept that. I'm not about to turn into someone like Donaldson. You may as well pound a stake through my chest right now or burn me at a stake—" Is that it? I can't think of any other ways I've read to kill vampires except—sunlight. I peer hard at Avery, a very tanned Avery who stood outside my gate in the full sun and seems not to have suffered any ill effect.

"Adaptation," he says.

"What?"

"It took hundreds of years, but we've adapted to sunlight. We can walk about in daylight just like anybody else, now."

My god. All the time I spent reading Anne Rice I thought I was reading fiction.

Avery holds up a hand. "You were reading fiction," he says. "For the most part. A stake through the heart or burning are ways we can be killed. There is also beheading, but that doesn't happen too much anymore. Mostly, if we're careful, we live long, productive lives and no one is the wiser."

"By long, you mean?"

He nods. "Immortality is part of the gift."

"But the blood thing—"

"I'm getting to that. The sources of energy used by living people—mostly connected to oxygen and food—

are closed off to us once the first stage of death begins. To replace what is used or lost in the course of our day is a regular source of fresh, arterial blood."

"I just said, I can't do that."

"You said you wouldn't turn into someone like Donaldson," he reminds me gently. "And you won't have to. I will teach you how to feed without killing. In fact, I will teach you how to feed in a way that will literally leave your hosts begging you not to stop."

"My host?"

He nods. "The living organism you draw from."

Great. I've turned into a parasite. "And I'm supposed to believe this host will enjoy the experience so much, he'll beg for more?"

Avery smiles. "Oh yes," he says. "Because while you're feeding, he'll be experiencing the very best sex he's ever had in his entire life."

CHAPTER 9

I T JUST GETS BETTER AND BETTER. NOW I'M A
parasite with nymphomaniacal tendencies. "And
where do I find these willing sex partners?" I ask,
though it's not really a question I want answered. I
wonder if I'll be working the homeless population or
frequenting bars down in Tijuana.

"Would you seek sex partners in those places under
normal circumstances?" he asks.

His voice contains a strong suggestion of reproach.
I lace my own with heavy sarcasm. "No. But I doubt
my boyfriend will take kindly to being drained of his
lifeblood on a daily basis."

"So you have sex daily?"

He's got a mocking grin on his face that I feel an ir-
resistible urge to smack right off.

Some of that feeling must convey itself to him

because he leans back out of reach. "Sorry," he says. "I don't mean to be impertinent. But you don't need to feed every day any more than you need to have sex every day. It's a matter of personal choice. Actually, in a short while you will need very little blood to sustain your new life force. A pint or so once a month will do it."

"You mean like the amount you donate at a blood bank?"

He understands the implication of what I'm asking and shakes his head. "Unfortunately, that blood is drawn from the veins and refrigerated. What you need to sustain life is fresh, arterial blood. You must drink directly from an artery in the neck or thigh."

I run my tongue over my teeth. With these? They feel the same. I remember Donaldson worrying at my neck until . . . the intense, breathtaking, wondrous pleasure of the experience floods back. My body tingles with the memory even now.

Stop it. I give myself a mental thump on the head. You can't do this.

Of course you can, Avery counters. *You just remembered how it was. And that was with a man who wasn't even trying to make it good for you. Think of what you do with your hands and body to give pleasure to your boyfriend. Then increase it by one thousand percent and you have an idea what magic you can work.*

But how do I hide the fact that I'm biting him? How do I know when to stop? What do I say when he notices the world's weirdest hickey on his neck?

God, I've just replied in kind without even thinking about it. I shake my head in dismay.

Avery waves a dismissive hand. *You'll get used to this. And your boyfriend won't notice anything other than a profoundly pleasurable sexual experience. You'll know when to stop because your body will tell you when it's had enough. As for the wound, it will disappear in a matter of minutes. All you have to do is lick it. Your saliva contains an alkaloid that will seal and heal the puncture; it's part of your physiology now.*

My hand goes to my neck. *Then why didn't my wound heal right away?*

Avery pushes himself off the couch. For the first time since I met him, he looks disturbed.

Donaldson didn't care if you found the wound or not. He intended that you die.

Like the woman he was living with.

Yes.

Avery drains the last of the water in the bottle and returns it to the kitchen.

I watch his departing back. There's something more he's waiting to tell me. I can't imagine how it can be worse than anything I've learned so far, but his reluctance to broach the subject makes me wonder.

He's back in the living room now, and his face is drawn and anxious. "I have more to tell you," he says.

"I figured as much," I reply dryly. "And it must be pretty bad if you're using your voice instead of . . . you know." I circle a finger at my head.

"It is." He doesn't sit down, but starts pacing up and

down in front of me. "Remember when I said I was a Night Watcher?"

I nod.

"And I told you I was one of a contingent of vampires who—"

"Monitors activity in a community, blah, blah, blah. Yeah. I remember. What does that have to do with me?"

"One of the things we watch for is renegade activity. A vampire like Donaldson, for instance, who attacks and kills without remorse and doesn't try to cover his crime. Sooner or later, the connection will be made between what he does and what he is. That makes him a threat to all of us."

"What do you a mean 'a threat'?"

"I mean, just as I am a watcher to protect our kind, there are others who seek to destroy us. They watch, too, for attacks that leave a victim bloodless. They have connections at police departments and hospitals, just as we have. And they pay a bounty for information leading to the identification of a vampire."

"You think they might be on to Donaldson?"

"Most definitely. But there's another consideration."

Avery pauses and the way he looks at me makes my skin crawl. "What?"

"If they know about Donaldson, they may know about you, too."

"Me?"

"Yes. You were attacked by Donaldson and lived. They will want to check you out, at the very least."

"And how will they do that?"

Avery shrugs. "It's hard to say. But you must be very careful how you conduct yourself. You will soon lose your hunger for regular food, but you must continue to shop as if you haven't. You must continue your normal routine. Be wary of strangers approaching you, and don't do anything to attract attention to yourself. If you feel the need to feed before your boyfriend returns, let me know. I'll help you find someone safe. In fact, it may be prudent to let me be there the first time you feed. You are at your most vulnerable then."

That picture—of Avery standing over me while I have sex—sends me into a paroxysm of laughter. The hysteria is back. "You're kidding," I sputter when I can finally calm myself. "You want to be there while I perform this unholy sex act on some poor, unsuspecting schmuck? Is that how you get your jollies? That's what this 'watcher' thing is all about?"

Once more, aggravation tightens Avery's mouth and darkens his eyes. "You should take this more seriously," he says, his voice hoarse with frustration. "I wasn't suggesting you feed for the first time while having sex. There are other alternatives. I just thought since you had a boyfriend, you would be relieved to know that you can maintain a monogamous relationship and safely satisfy your hunger, too."

Oh, yes. That's an immense relief. The ultimate safe sex. Max will be so pleased.

He can be.

God.

Avery is in my head again. I'm too tired to fight it, but something else he said about feeding sifts through.

"What do you mean I'm the most vulnerable when I feed?"

Avery comes back to the couch and reclaims his seat at the end of it. "In the beginning," he says. "You may be so swept up in the excitement—"

Excitement?

Yes. You don't understand now. But you will. Anyway, there have been cases where our enemies have pretended to be seduced by a new vampire, only to stake him or her during the act. As you gain experience, you learn to sense the danger.

More animal instincts to be developed. Great.

I look over at Avery. *I think you should go now.*

Avery watches me for a long minute. I don't even try to read his thoughts. I just want to be alone with mine.

He pushes himself to his feet. "I'm sorry this is so hard on you," he says.

"And you thought it wouldn't be?"

He rolls his shoulders. "Most people choose to become," he says. "It's the only safe way. Occasionally, someone like you has it forced on them. I don't know how to make it better except to assure you that there are others like myself to help you through the transition."

"Wonderful. A fanged support group. Just what I've always wanted."

"Give it a few days," he says, ignoring the sarcasm. "You will start to feel the change. And you will realize there are some good things—some very good things— that come with the gift."

"Gift? That's how you see it?"

He smiles, a soft, sweet smile. "It's how you will see

it, too, eventually. You must, really, if you are to go on."

Go on? Ah, that's the rub, isn't it? Will I choose to go on?

I STAY ON THE COUCH AFTER AVERY LEAVES. HE seemed reluctant to go, after catching my last thought, but finally he did. Now I'm stretched out, watching rays of a dying sun filter through the window and thinking of a hundred other questions I should have asked him. My knowledge of vampire lore comes from books. Works of fiction, or so I thought. Now I realize that, as in most folk tales, there is always a grain of truth. I wonder how many of those books were actually written by vampires? How many vampire cousins do I have? Are there enclaves of vampires in various communities? Is there a secret handshake or sign to identify one vampire to the other?

Vampire.

I'm rolling the word around my tongue and around my brain, trying to make sense of what Avery says is now my reality. I have been given the "gift" of immortality with just one small drawback. I have to drink the blood of unsuspecting humans to sustain that life. Even though Avery painted a titillating picture of wild sexual gratification bestowed on willing victims, they are victims nonetheless. I can't imagine subjecting Max to that. I won't.

So, what to do now?

I close my eyes and put a cushion over my face.

But the darkness isn't quite dark enough.

I get a picture of Avery, tan and good-looking. Normal-looking even. So much for the pale, delicate-skinned vampire who doesn't venture out into the sunlight. Obviously, that's one of the myths perpetuated by books and movies. How did all that get started? And why hasn't the truth come out before now? And then there's that aversion to garlic—

Oh boy.

The lasagna.

Well, I won't make that mistake again. Obviously, some of those folk tales have a basis in fact. That's going to be a hard one, though, giving up Italian food. Especially Luigi's, where the motto is if you don't like garlic, stay home.

But soon I'll be giving up all food, right? Isn't that what Avery said?

The ringing of a telephone interrupts my chain of thought. With a weary sigh, I hoist myself off the couch and trudge over to answer it.

"Well," a familiar voice tinged with irritation starts right in. "Who the hell is he, Anna? Who's the guy I just saw leave your house?"

"Max?"

"You haven't answered my question."

I cross to the window and look toward the street. "Where are you?"

A figure steps out from the driver's side of a parked car with dark-tinted windows. "Here. See me?"

I nod before I realize he can't see *me*. "What are you doing out there? Come in."

"Are you alone?"

"Yes. I'm alone. You can relax those secret agent muscles. Now, will you get your ass in here, or do I come out and get you?"

The handsome face splits into a wide grin I can see even from here.

"I was hoping you'd say that. I'm on my way."

CHAPTER 10

I'T'S A REFLEX ACTION, RUSHING INTO MAX'S arms the moment he appears at the door. He's big and strong and exudes a quiet masculinity that won me over the moment we met. Add to that the allure of tan Latin skin, dark hair and eyes the color of the ocean in the morning, and for a moment, there's nothing except the feel of his body against mine. The electric touch of his fingers on my neck as he kisses me. I curl into the curve of his body, flesh against flesh, man against woman.

He kicks the door shut with his foot and maneuvers me to the couch.

We fall upon it, breathless, eager.

Then I remember.

It's not exactly man against woman anymore.

"Max." I push against his chest with my hands, forcing him to stop and look at me.

He does. But his eyes. Those eyes. I almost lose myself again. But I can't. Already I feel my body responding in such an intense way, if I hesitate now, we might both be lost. "Wait."

He sits back a little, a puzzled smile tweaking the corners of his mouth. He seems to notice what I have on for the first time.

"Is this a new look?" he asks, running a finger along the neckline of the scrubs. "Hospital chic the new rage this season?"

Then he looks at my face, really looks at me, for the first time. His smile freezes, melts away. His finger traces the cut at my hairline. "Are you hurt? What happened to you?"

I know most of my injuries have faded, only the hint of a cut where Donaldson first hit me remains. And? My hand goes to the wound at my throat. But I feel nothing except a small bump of raised skin. I let Max help me into a sitting position beside him on the couch.

"I got into a little trouble a couple of nights ago."

"A little trouble? How little?"

I move away from him slightly so I can face him squarely. "A skip we were working jumped us."

"Jumped you and David?"

He's frowning now. I feel his body tense, and I put a gentle hand on his arm. "We're okay. Just banged up. The guy you saw leaving? That was the doctor who treated me."

But that bit of news doesn't bring about the response I'd hoped. Max's frown deepens. "Jesus, Anna.

The doctor came here to check up on you? It must have been pretty serious."

"No, not really." I don't want to tell Max any more than I have to. I start to babble. "I was released from the hospital today. He was in the neighborhood, that's all. And don't look so worried. David is fine. He's with Gloria in L.A., so you know he wasn't hurt that bad either. I'm just still a little sore. Guess I bruised a rib or two. Anyway, I'm supposed to take it easy for a week or so."

It sounds lame, even to my ears, but I can't think of any other way to avoid the inevitable. I can't have sex with Max until I learn how to control this thing.

Until I learn how to control this thing?

I'm actually considering Avery's suggestion?

I pull away from Max and get to my feet. I can't trust myself to be this close. I know Max is watching me intently. I feel a familiar tingling in the pit of my stomach, an unwelcome surge of excitement even lower.

"Bruised ribs?" Max is on his feet, too. "Your ribs didn't seem to be hurting a minute ago."

Why did I say bruised ribs? I start to turn away, but Max turns me back. "There's more, isn't there?" His voice is soft and concerned. "What did he do to you, Anna?"

I hesitate and blow out a breath. We had sex, and he turned me into a vampire. "Nothing, Max. Really. I'm more embarrassed than hurt. But I'm just not feeling quite right yet." I press a hand to my forehead. "My head still hurts, and it's making me a little woozy."

He doesn't believe me; I see it on his face. But he

remains silent, contemplative. Finally, he leads me back to the couch, and we sit down side by side. After another long moment, I steal a sideways glance at him. He's watching me.

"David is in L.A.?" he says.

I nod. "With Gloria." I know suddenly why he's asking. "You aren't going to bother him, Max," I say firmly. "I'm telling you it was nothing. We're both going to be just fine."

"And what did you say that doctor's name was?"

"I didn't."

Max stirs, picking up a pillow and laying it back down.

He's irritated.

I can't say that I blame him. I just can't do anything about it. The way I usually work him out of a bad mood isn't an option at this particular time.

"Max, come on." I put a hand on his shoulder. "Talk to me. How's the job going? I heard about a big bust in the Southeast last week. I figured it was one of yours."

He doesn't answer right away. I start to think he's not going to answer at all and then he exhales noisily and places his hand over mine. "The job is going great," he says. "The bust was one of the biggest ever. Now there's only the money trail and we can wrap this thing up."

He shifts a little on the couch, raises my hand and brushes the palm against his lips. It's all I can do to keep from purring. Instead, though, I give him a little "go on" bob of my head.

He sighs and continues. "This afternoon I drove the

boss over the border to visit his mama. When I dropped him off, he gave me five hundred bucks and told me to get laid." He reaches into his pocket and pulls out the wad of cash. "Hold this for me, will you? If I go back with this, he'll know I didn't get laid. Of course, it looks like I'm not going to get laid anyway, so what difference does it make, huh?"

I give him the look. "So, that's the only reason you come to see me? Sex is the only attraction?"

He capitulates with a smile. "Not the *only* attraction," he says. "But when I haven't seen you in two months and I don't know when I'll see you again and we only have a few hours . . . Well, it's hardly enough time to enter into a comprehensive discussion of world politics, is it?" He leans toward me, his lips dangerously close. "But it's certainly enough time to explore other interesting topics. Things like breasts." His left hand cups my right breast. "Or thighs." His hand moves down.

Then his lips move past my cheek and blow gently into my ear. "I could be very, very gentle, Anna."

My defenses slip away. Sex with Max is one of the great pleasures of my life. The fact that we see each other only sporadically, and always unexpectedly, adds to the delight.

But I can't do this now. I don't trust myself. Regretfully, I pull away. "Please, Max. I just don't feel well."

"Oh. Headache, huh?"

I nod and do the palm to the forehead thing again.

He laughs. "It isn't working, Anna," he says. "You're the toughest woman I know. And you're wired for sex like nobody I've ever met. So, are you going to tell me what's really going on here? Or do I have to track down David and get the truth from him?"

It's an empty threat. Max's undercover work as a driver for one of Mexico's most notorious gangsters keeps him on a short leash. In fact, his assignment is how we met. Not long after I got into the business, a skip I was working agreed to turn informant in exchange for a get-out-of-jail-free card. The Feds became very interested when they learned the guy was a lieutenant in the gangster's mob. I arranged the deal and Max turned out to be the plant. So I know for sure he won't be making any unscheduled forays into L.A. to question David.

And Max knows it, too, but I give him points for the effort.

When I don't respond, he sighs. "Okay. I give up. I don't know what's wrong, but I can't force you to tell me. I'm not buying this injured act, and I can't believe anybody could get the best of you and David. But I've trusted you with my life since the first moment I saw you. I guess I just have to trust that whatever is bothering you now has nothing to do with us."

It's a touching speech. I believe he believes what he's saying. I also *know* Max lies for a living, and his acting skills are what have kept him alive in some pretty tough situations. I wipe an imaginary tear from my eye.

We both start laughing at the same time.

"So," he says, coming up for air. "Got anything to eat? I'm starved."

I take his hand and pull him toward the kitchen.

"I don't suppose you have anything from Luigi's," he says, scanning the contents of my refrigerator. "I'd kill for a plate of his lasagna."

CHAPTER 11

I T'S TEN O'CLOCK. MAX LEFT TO PICK UP HIS
boss, and I'm staring at the pile of dirty dishes in the
sink. Do vampires really have to do their own dishes?
I've never seen one do that in movies.

I rinse the dishes, load them into the dishwasher,
and reach for the Cascade. The phone on the counter
rings so loudly it makes me jump. The box slips from
my hand, and before I can catch it, powder spills across
the floor.

Shit. The second time today I've made a mess.

Do I have to avoid loud noises, too? Is that another
vampire bogey?

Before I can say hello, he begins. "Anna, this is Grant
Avery. Sorry to disturb you. Is your friend still there?"

Now I'm getting mad. "Doesn't anyone say hello
anymore? And if you know I had someone here, then
you know he's gone. So why are you asking?"

"Sorry."

His tone is unapologetic and quite insincere, but it's something else that triggers alarm bells in my head. "Avery, please tell me that you aren't having him followed."

There's a slight hesitation before he replies. "No, it's not Max we're having followed."

Max? He knows his name? The alarms are shrieking now. "Avery, can you read my thoughts over the phone?"

He starts talking in the same dry, academic pitch he used when explaining my new "gift."

"No, actually I can't," he says. "Something about electric circuits that interfere. If you're wondering how I knew Max's name, it popped into your thoughts once or twice while I was there this afternoon."

For the first time, I'm disappointed to hear that he can't get inside my head. In fact, I'm fighting a wave of panic. "Can you come over now? Or can I come to you? We have to talk about Max."

"Well," he says, "that's convenient because I have something to talk to you about, also. Would you like to come here?"

"And here is?"

"Do you know the Mount Soledad area?"

Everyone on the coast knows the Mount Soledad area. It's one of the most prestigious addresses in prestigious La Jolla. A vampire doctor. Figures that's where he'd live. "Want to give me the address?"

I reach for a piece of paper and write it down. "I can be there in twenty minutes."

"Good. And Anna?"

"Yes?"

"Wear something nice. I have some folks I'd like you to meet."

And he hangs up.

I replace the receiver, frowning at both the implication and inflection of his tone. I have a good mind to come as I am, in the scrubs he so graciously lent me when I left the hospital.

But on the other hand, maybe I'm about to meet some of my vampire relatives. First impressions are always important, aren't they?

FOR WORK, I DRIVE A FORD CROWN VIC, THE SAME model as most cops and tricked out with a lot of the same gadgets. For pleasure, I drive a two-year-old, British Racing Green Jag XKR convertible. Between the car payment and insurance, I shell out what amounts to the mortgage on a small house each month. But it's my only luxury, and since I own the cottage outright, it's a concession I'm able to make.

As I pull into Dr. Avery's driveway, I'm sure that at least my car will fit in with this crowd. I park between a silver Lexus and a big Mercedes sedan. And did I say driveway? I climb out of my car and glance back along a tree-lined avenue that meanders about a half mile from a gated entrance to the front of the stone mansion.

Pretty damned impressive, even for this neighborhood. Either medicine or vampirism pays very well.

Dr. Avery answers the doorbell himself. He's all

spiffed up in a navy suit with a cream shirt and red silk tie. Black basket weave oxfords peek from beneath the cuffs of tailored slacks. Even his mop of hair lies tamed and moussed. He looks every inch the country gentleman.

I raise an eyebrow. *I expected a servant to answer the door.*

The servants have the night off, he says, ushering me in with a hand on my back. *Welcome to my home. You look wonderful, too, by the way.*

Did I say he looked wonderful? I have to be more careful with my thoughts. And it makes me wonder what I was thinking when I decided to come to Avery. I can't protect *myself* from creatures who can invade my thoughts at will. How can I hope to protect Max? What I need to tell Avery, I need to tell him in private. Max's safety depends on it.

Max is safe, Avery assures me. *Remember, the thoughts of my guests will be as open to you as yours are to them. We all have secrets.*

But that doesn't make me feel any better as he guides me through an immense foyer and into a living room with more square footage than my entire house. One wall is floor to ceiling windows and another is a huge stone fireplace big enough for a man to walk into. There is a small cluster of people gathered in a tight knot in front of a roaring fire. I count six, three men and three women, talking in soft voices, seemingly unaware of our approach.

The men are all in their mid-forties, wearing suits of gray or dark blue. Their intense faces are ruggedly handsome; their bodies under the exquisitely tailored clothes look lean and fit. The women are similarly attired in Armani and Gucci, with glittering stones in their earlobes and at their throats. They all sip from martini glasses and wave well-manicured hands to make their points.

They are the people you see on the society pages and in the glossy magazines. I recognize several, including the deputy mayor of San Diego and the chief of police.

No wonder Avery said my secrets would be safe.

There is a break in conversation, and Avery urges me to join the group. But I feel as out of my element as my off-the-rack outfit is to the designer suits in front of me.

Avery's voice comes from behind me and I jump.

You look wonderful, he says a second time. *That color is perfect with your hair and complexion and silk flatters your figure. You are a beautiful woman, Anna. Don't worry that you can't compete.*

I was thinking about my clothes, I reply archly. *I have never worried about competing.*

He smiles.

Well, I haven't, I repeat. It sounds childish, even to my ears.

God, what if *they* heard?

So much for first impressions. My eyes turn back to the group, but talk seems to have resumed, and no one is looking our way. If they picked up on any of that, it's not apparent. I touch Avery's arm.

Can we go somewhere else to talk? I gesture toward the fireplace. *I'm not ready for this yet.*

He looks a little disappointed, but he doesn't try to dissuade me. Instead, he leads me back out to the foyer, where he heads to the right and toward a pair of carved wooden double doors. He passes in front of me to swing one of the doors open, and I follow him in.

This is the library.

I raise an eyebrow at him. *No kidding? Is that what you call a room with hundreds of books? A library? I'm glad you cleared that up. Avery, I may live on the other side of the tracks in Mission Beach, but I do read.*

He doesn't appreciate my sarcasm. I can't catch what he's thinking, but there's no mistaking the set of his jaw or the suggestion of annoyance hovering in his eyes.

I can't catch what he's thinking. Why is that?

"I'm sorry," I say aloud. "I'm a little nervous."

The apology does the trick. He relaxes, physically and mentally, and opens his mind to me once again.

You have to teach me to do that, I tell him, shaking a finger. *You didn't mention that you can shut yourself down when you want, did you?*

A faint light sparkles in the depths of those green eyes. *I'm not going to divulge all my secrets right away. Otherwise, you won't need me anymore. Would you like a drink?*

Red wine, if you have it.

This time he raises an eyebrow. *I think I can find something you'll like.*

He moves away from me and toward a large sideboard. With a push of a button, a door slides open. Inside the lighted cabinet, crystal decanters wink and sparkle like so many jewels on a bed of velvet. He chooses one, pours two glasses, and beckons me to follow him.

We find ourselves on a wide balcony hovering over the dark Pacific many feet below. I can't see anything except the vast emptiness of the ocean, but I can hear the waves.

He hands me a glass. *Hope you like this. It's from my family's vineyards.*

Oh, you're from Napa Valley?

He has the glass to his lips, but just stops himself from taking a sip as a gurgle of laughter erupts. *No*, he says, *not Napa. Provence.*

Provence? As in France?

He smiles. It's the same kind of smile I used to give slow students.

Okay. So I forgot for a minute that you're probably a thousand years old with roots that go back to the Stone Age. I told you, I'm not quite with the program yet. You have to cut me some slack.

Avery still has that smile on his face, but he's taken a seat on a patio chair and motions with his glass for me to join him.

I take a seat opposite him and raise my glass for the first taste of a wine I suspect I'll never be able to afford. I don't expect to like it, either, so I'm quite caught off guard by the sublime flavor. It's rich and dry and tastes elemental, as though made of earth and sea as well as grape. I take a second sip and smile.

You like it.

I do. And yes, I'm surprised. I've never been a connoisseur of wines. I don't have the pallet for it, or so I've always thought.

I raise the glass. *Or is this another acquired vampire thing? Blood and wine, elixirs of life?*

Avery laughs, tilting his head as he watches me over the top of his glass. *No, it's not a vampire thing. Not really. But you will find you've misjudged a lot of things, Anna.*

His eyes lock me in their gaze for a long moment. I can't read him again, but suddenly something vaguely sensual passes between us.

I pull myself away, and stand up. *This isn't what I came here for.*

He stands, too. *I know. You came to talk about Max.*

Max. Yes. Just saying his name snaps me back. I look toward the windows across from us and into the living room, where the fire reflecting on the glass catches two figures in stark relief. A man and a woman. Vampires cast no reflection. Avery has invited humans to meet me?

Startled, I turn to Avery, *They aren't all vampires?*

He shakes his head. *No. The wife of Police Chief Williams and the husband of Deputy Mayor Davis are mortal.*

I look back at the two. *Do they know—?*

That their spouses are vampire? Yes, of course.

And they accept it?

What they accept is a life bountiful beyond their wildest dreams. It is the vampire who suffers in such a union.

It's not what I expected to hear. I turn to look at him. Avery's face is set, his eyes hooded. *You don't approve.*

It's not my place to approve or disapprove, he retorts shortly.

But why did you say it's the vampire who suffers?

He turns his face away from me. *You will learn the answer to that on your own.*

He returns to the library and the sideboard where he pours himself another glass of wine. He doesn't offer me a second glass or return to the balcony. He takes a seat behind a large desk in the middle of the room and waits for me to join him inside.

I don't understand the abrupt change in his attitude and demeanor, but he's shut himself off from me again, and I have no choice. I answer the summons.

He waits for me to take a seat across from him before beginning.

We have important things to discuss. It's getting late and I must return to my guests. If you don't wish to accompany me, I suggest we get down to business.

I nod, but my paranoia springs back. *How do I know the people in the other room can't hear us?*

Avery tilts his head. *Listen.*

I do. Soft music, classical, something low and sweet drifts on the air from hidden speakers. I listen harder. Below the music, a hum. *White noise?*

He nods.

Prevents thought transference from room to room. I value my privacy. I protect that of my guests.

That electrical circuit thing you mentioned?

He nods again.

I hesitate, but for just a moment. I have to trust Avery.

Max is an undercover agent with the DEA. His life depends on keeping our relationship a secret. He only visits me when it's absolutely safe. I never know when he'll show up, so I need to know how you found out about his visit.

Avery purses his lips. He's closed his mind, so I can only wait until he's ready to reply. But the fact that, all of a sudden, this mind reading is a one-way street is beginning to grate. I make it a point to let him know it.

You'll learn the trick soon enough, he fires back. *Now do you want an answer to your question?*

I swallow down the caustic retort I want to fling across at him and just say, *Yes.*

You are the one being watched.

Me? Why?

I told you this afternoon. You may be in danger. You don't have all your powers yet. It's our custom to protect fledglings, so to speak, until they find their wings.

And you didn't think it important to tell me this?

Would you have approved?

Of course not. I can take care of myself.

The way you did with Donaldson?

He throws it out like a challenge, his eyes flashing.

Now my irritation bubbles over and erupts into full-blown anger. "Donaldson was a fluke. David and I have handled much worse and come out on top. Vampire or no, we would have had him if things hadn't gotten so crazy."

"Oh, you think so?"

Before I can draw a breath, Avery is up and out of his

chair. He sweeps me from mine and I am pinned under his body on the floor. I can't move my hands or my legs. His weight is crushing. His lips are at my ear and he whispers, "Can you take me?"

I don't understand what's happening. Avery is strong, stronger even than Donaldson. But there's nothing sexual in this attack. Does he mean to kill me?

I can't read his thoughts. His breath is ragged in my ear. I feel his mouth at my neck.

Suddenly, something changes.

His neck is there, a pulsing heartbeat, in reach. Panic becomes a lust from his blood. He eases his grip and I pull an arm free, yanking at his tie until it loosens, ripping at the top button of his shirt until it gives way. With animal instinct, I tear at him. I snap and gnaw with my teeth until the skin breaks and there is a glorious rush of adrenaline-laced fire coursing down my throat. He tastes of wine and sunshine and I work a hand free to hold his head captive while I drink.

I drink.

A fragment of a thought breaks through.

Anna, enough.

But I clutch at Avery, drawing him even closer. *I don't want to stop.*

You must.

Avery is now lying very still. He does not try to pull away. His mind is open, a feeling of euphoria radiating from him like heat from the sun. He is calmly waiting for me to make the decision.

I think that's what saves him. I drop my head back onto the carpet, awash with guilt and shame. What have I done?

Avery shifts his weight and looks down at me for a long moment. Then he lifts himself off me, and holds out a hand to help me up.

You did what I wanted you to do, he says.

CHAPTER 12

*Y*OU WANTED THIS TO HAPPEN?
  Avery still has my hand. He guides me back to the chair and I sink into it. He returns to the sideboard and pours another glass of wine. Holding it out to me, he asks, *How do you feel?*

I take the glass, but I don't drink. Instead, I place it on the desk, my mind reeling with the implications of what I've done. I look over at Avery. He's holding a hand against his neck as if it hurts. There's blood on his collar.

"I didn't want to stop."

He smiles.

"What if I hadn't? What if I'd drained you?"

But you didn't.

"But I might have. The sensation, the *pleasure* of feeding . . . I don't know that I will always be able to stop."

His smile widens. *You can, Anna, and you will. That's why this happened.*

Avery leans toward me. *You needed to feed. The blood of an old soul is the most powerful and I knew you weren't likely to feed on your own. I wanted you to see that it is instinctive to feed, just as instinctive as it once was to breathe. And I wanted you to realize that you do not have to hurt or kill your host to satisfy your own needs.*

But you are not mortal. You could have stopped me, I know that. You are much more powerful than I am.

For now. Your power is growing.

But what if it had been a man?

You mean, what if it had been Max?

Yes.

Whose voice did you hear telling you to stop?

My own. I realize. *It was my own.*

He smiles again. *Your instincts kicked in as I knew they would. Becoming does not alter the type of person you are. Good or evil still exists for us. Just as you have a heartbeat, you also have a soul. You are a good person, Anna. That will not change. Only your physical realities are altered.*

Then what happened to Donaldson? He had no prior history of violence in his record. How did he turn into a killer?

Avery shrugs. *The image Donaldson projected to the world was much different than the reality. He had a dark side. Unfortunately, becoming for him meant unleashing that dark side.*

He pushes back from the desk and his expression

hardens. His eyes become flat and, once again, unreadable. He studies me for a long moment before the spark of some indefinable emotion flares and his mind opens.

I'm glad you've been thinking of Donaldson.

I sniff. *How could I not?*

Do you understand what I've explained to you about the gift? Do you accept the reality?

Do I have a choice?

"You always have a choice," he says aloud. "The question is what you choose to do with your life as it now is."

My life as it now is.

It's such a simple statement, and yet it hits me with the force of a lightning bolt. Maybe it's because I haven't had time yet to truly digest all that's happened. Maybe it's because there's some small part of me that still thinks this is a dream and I'll awaken and everything will be the same as before. Whatever the reason, I don't know what to say.

Avery nods, picking through my conflicting thoughts and emotions and responding to them. *That's understandable. And I wish you had the luxury of taking your time to sort it all out. But you don't, Anna.*

His tone is sad and his eyes are full of concern.

It scares me. "Why do you say that?"

Avery stands and moves away from the desk. He goes to a closet where he pulls out a fresh shirt from an armoire inside. As if oblivious to my presence, he takes off his coat and tie, removes the soiled shirt and slips on a clean one. He leaves the tie on the desk, but he puts his jacket back on. All the while, his thoughts are carefully sealed away from me.

For the first time, I don't want to know what he's thinking. Fear coils around my thoughts and in the pit of my stomach. After all I've been through, what could be so terrible that he hesitates to tell me? All the remarkable strength I felt after feeding evaporates with the dread building in my chest, because I realize that whatever it is, he doesn't think I can handle it.

And that makes me mad.

"Avery."

He turns from the window, surprised at the sound of my voice—or rather, at my tone.

"How dare you do this to me? I've gone along with all your stupid games. I've listened to your words of wisdom and accepted what you've told me I must accept. But I won't let you make me afraid. Either you tell me what's got you so spooked, or I walk out of here right now and I don't come back."

His mouth pulls into a sour grin. "You think you are prepared to go your own way?"

"You just told me that I was. You just told me that I'm still the same person, that it's my body, not my mind that has changed. If that's true, I don't need you to live as I always have."

A glint of amusement returns to his eyes. But his mind is still closed.

And that must stop, too.

He tweaks an eyebrow at me.

I mean it, Avery. Either you open your mind to me fully and all the time, or I shut my thoughts away from you, too.

You think you can?

I watch his face as I do.

He doesn't believe it, at first. He keeps his eyes on mine, tries to bore into my head. I refuse to look away or to allow him access. After a moment, I smile.

It's not so hard, is it?

He smiles back. *How did you figure it out?*

By being observant. You do this thing with your eyes when you shut down. You narrow them just a bit at the corners. I thought I'd try it, too. Guess it works, huh?

I soften my tone. *Now, can we get down to whatever it is that has you so upset. Just give it to me straight.*

Avery gestures me back to the desk. *All right, Anna. Sit down, please.*

I settle myself in.

You want it straight, here it is. You have to find Donaldson. And you have to kill him.

CHAPTER 13

MAYBE I SHOULDN'T HAVE ASKED HIM TO BE so direct. A laugh bubbles up. "You're kidding, right?"

Does it feel like I'm kidding?

The urge to laugh dissipates like air from a popped balloon. *No. It doesn't. But it also doesn't make sense. Two minutes ago you told me I wasn't like Donaldson. Now you're telling me to find him and kill him.*

He pauses, a heartbeat, then, "Have you watched any television tonight? Heard any news on the radio?"

I shake my head.

Avery's eyes are grim as his frown deepens. He places his elbows on the desk and leans toward me. *Donaldson has killed again. Two more victims were found near the border. He's getting more daring and more careless. Chief Williams has managed to keep most of the details from the press, but it won't be long before someone leaks the fact that there's a killer out there draining his victims' blood.*

I'm on my feet, pacing in front of the desk. *But the police are looking for Donaldson. They'll find him and bring him in.*

It's not our way.

What?

We have to take care of our own, Anna. We can't risk his bringing attention to our community. Remember, I told you there are people out there who seek to destroy us. Donaldson's victims are just what these people look for. Even with Chief Williams' influence, these killings will not go unnoticed.

And my tracking him down and killing him will be?

If you're careful.

Suspicion replaces surprise in the back of my mind, especially since Avery is carefully guarding his thoughts. I let the doubt seep into my voice. "Is this a setup?"

He looks puzzled. "A setup? What do you mean?"

I wave a hand at the door. "I mean I wasn't invited to join your little flock. Maybe sending me after Donaldson is a way to get rid of me."

"If I wanted to get rid of you, Anna, I could have killed you in the hospital. You had lost a lot of blood. I could have easily drained you of the rest, and no one would have been the wiser."

The abruptness of his reply gives it a ring of truth and his thoughts confirm it.

"Then why choose me to do this? Surely, there are others better qualified."

He looks at me as if I've asked a very stupid question. "Weren't you tracking Donaldson down when he attacked you? Isn't this what you do for a living?"

It's my turn to stare at him. "With a big difference. When I was tracking Donaldson, it was with the intention of turning him over to the authorities. I am willing to do that again, but I won't kill him."

Now, in spite of what he's just asked me to do, his thoughts reflect skepticism about my ability to bring Donaldson in.

I feel warmth flood my face, knowing that he's remembering how easily he overpowered me just moments before.

I will be ready this time.

He raises an eyebrow. *And Donaldson will be ready for you.*

How will Donaldson know?

Avery's green eyes narrow. *You and he have a connection. He will be able to feel your presence long before he will be able to see you. You will be able to hide your thoughts from him, but he will sense you nonetheless. You can use that to your advantage, but it can be dangerous, too.*

How so?

The drawback is that he will know that there is someone close that he has turned. If you are careful to keep your thoughts from him, he will not know who it is. So far, we have been successful in keeping your name out of both police and press reports. He knows he was interrupted with you, but at the rate he's killing, he may not notice that you have been omitted from his list of victims.

And the advantages?

You will be able to sense him, too. You will know where he has been. If you hone in on his thoughts, you will know where he is going. You can set a trap—

There is a discreet knock at the door. Avery pushes himself away from the desk and crosses the room. He opens the door just wide enough to allow him to greet his visitor without revealing my presence.

It's Police Chief Williams. His thoughts are troubled. *They've found another body. I must go.*

I watch Avery reach out a hand. *We'll take care of this. Be assured.*

Williams sighs. *We'd better. We haven't had trouble like this in a long time. I like it here, Avery. I don't want to be forced to move because of this renegade. He must be dealt with.*

Avery moves out of the room for a moment, pulling the door shut behind him. Then he reappears and, once more, closes the door.

I assume the maneuver was to prevent me from hearing his parting shot to the police chief. It doesn't matter. I've already made up my mind.

I get to my feet. "I'm leaving, too, Avery."

He tries to probe my mind. When he doesn't succeed, he frowns, eyes hard. *You are choosing not to help?*

"I am choosing to protect myself. You have a nice little support group here of many of San Diego's most prominent citizens. The way I see it, inviting me tonight was a way to dangle the carrot. I can become a part of this exclusive club if I perform one little task for you.

The trouble is, as the newest member, I am also the most expendable. If I kill Donaldson, so much the better. If Donaldson kills me, I don't upset the balance of power. You can probably find another newly minted vampire to take my place. You say this isn't a setup. Forgive me if I find that hard to believe."

Avery has grown very still. He listens intently, brows furrowed, allowing nothing of what he's feeling to come through.

It confirms that my read on the situation is correct. I move to meet him at the door and he finally opens his thoughts.

I can't force you to do this, Anna.

His tone is soft, almost seductive.

I know. That's why I'm leaving.

I won't stop you.

Avery steps back from the door. *My home is forever open to you. As time goes on, you will have questions. I am, and always will be, at your service.*

He sounds so formal, like he's reciting an official vampire ceremonial closing speech.

He smiles at my interpretation. *Well, after three hundred years, we'll see how dated you sound.*

THAT WAS FAR TOO EASY.

I've got the top down on the Jag and I'm cruising west on Ardath toward home. Avery didn't try to talk me into his plan or out of leaving.

Neither of which makes sense.

But it's one in the morning, the night is cloudless

and the road is deserted. I want to shake off the feeling of Avery and his band of merry vampires, so I give the Jag its head. There's nothing like the acceleration of an 8 cylinder, 390 hp supercharged engine to clear away the cobwebs.

I should know better.

The cop picks me up at the intersection of Torrey Pines and Ardath. I see him the same time he sees me, and I know that little radar gun he's pointed at me has already registered the fact that I'm speeding by at 120 mph. There's no sense in reaching for the emergency brake to try to throw him off. I simply take my foot off the gas and let the black and white catch up.

He does, lights flashing. I pull over and wait for him to come to me. I've worked with cops long enough to know you don't jump out of your car or start rummaging in your purse for your license. It makes them testy. So I sit quietly, both hands on the steering wheel like a good little girl, and watch in the rearview mirror as he approaches. He's big, thick bodied, like a wrestler, with his cap pulled down low over his face.

He shines a flashlight in my eyes. "Good morning, Miss. Do you know why I stopped you?"

On reflex, I put up a hand to shield my eyes. "I was speeding."

He doesn't lower the flashlight. "Please put your hands back on the steering wheel."

"Please lower the flashlight. It's hurting my eyes."

He doesn't drop the light, but instead shoves it closer to my face. The glare causes sharp pinpricks of pain at the back of my eyes. Is this another vampire peculiarity? I can go out in sunlight, but the strobe of a flashlight is intolerable?

I hear, rather than see, my car door being opened. The cop's voice is hard and brittle at my ear. "Please step out of the car," he says.

I do, stumbling a little. It's as if the light is affecting my equilibrium as well as my sight.

"Have you been drinking, Miss?"

God. I assume he means alcohol. How much wine did I drink? I remember one glass. It's probably not wise to share that though. "No, officer. I haven't been drinking. It's that light in my eyes that's causing the problem. Is it really necessary to blind me?"

He must take umbrage at my tone, because before I can say anything else, his hands dig into my shoulders and he's turning me so that I'm facing my car. He jerks my hands together behind my back.

"I'm afraid I'm going to have to take you in," he says, snapping cuffs on my wrists.

It happens so fast that I don't have time to react. "You're *arresting* me?" I squeak, outrage notching my voice up an octave. "For what?"

I still haven't seen his face. I try to turn but he doesn't let me.

"Driving under the influence, Miss," he says, shoving me toward his car.

I dig my heels in. "Wait a minute. Don't you have to give me a sobriety test or something? I tell you, I'm not drunk."

But even if I were, the muzzle of the gun pressed into the small of my back would have sobered me up fast enough. "What are you doing?"

"Get into the car, bitch," he says, his voice full of venom. "Or I'll stake you right here."

CHAPTER 14

HE'S HUMAN; I FEEL IT. ONE OF THOSE ANTI-watchers Avery warned me about? I stop fighting and let him manhandle me into the backseat of the car. I don't know what a bullet will do to me, and I'm not sure this is the time to find out. I figure my best chance to get away will be when we get to wherever it is he plans to take me. I'm willing to bet it won't be jail.

He's stopped talking. He sweeps the cap off his head and tosses it into the passenger seat. Then he's behind the wheel. He throws me an over-the-shoulder glance through the mesh of the wire partition separating us. "Relax," he says. "We're going for a ride."

I settle back into the seat, working at the cuffs. They're standard police issue. If I had my purse, I could use my own handcuff key to free myself. Unfortunately, it's in the trunk of my car.

"Aren't you going to let me get my purse?" I ask. "It's in the car."

He ignores the request as he guides the police car back onto the road. He makes a U-turn at the first opportunity, and we're soon cruising north on Torrey Pines Road. Away from downtown San Diego and jail.

"Where are you taking me?"

I may as well be talking to myself. Once again, he doesn't answer. He doesn't even act as if he's heard.

"Somewhere dark and deserted, I imagine," I continue anyway. "You'll need privacy for what you have in mind. Around here that would be what—Torrey Pines State Park?"

His eyes flash back in the mirror, but of course I don't show up there—and he stops looking.

But I can see him. The streetlights cast enough illumination for me to study his face. He's younger than I am, with short-cropped blond hair and a jutting chin. "Are you even a real cop?"

That brings a smile to his full lips. "Yeah. I'm a real cop. I'm here to protect and serve. Getting rid of vermin like you is my favorite part of the job."

I think back to what Avery said. "And you get a bounty for each vampire you dust, right? How do you prove the kill? Is there a little red Dustbuster back here somewhere?"

"You're a real smart-ass, aren't you?" The blue eyes harden. "They'll find your car tomorrow morning. Your ID is inside. When it's learned that you've vanished, that will be all the confirmation I need."

"So it's only been forty-eight hours, and I've already

been identified as a vampire," I say. "I'm impressed. How do you get your information?"

But he doesn't reply. In fact, the rest of the ride he remains silent, doesn't even glance back again. So I use the time to test the cuffs, twisting my wrists to see if I can slip my hands out. No dice. I try to wriggle myself down in the seat, thinking if I can maneuver my hands in front, I'll have a better chance to defend myself. But I can't do that without making it obvious what I'm up to, and then I'll lose the element of surprise.

I remain slouched, watching his eyes in the mirror. The mirror. I can see him but he can't see me. I've transformed enough to have lost my reflection. Let's see if I can make that work for me.

I've never been especially limber. I take yoga more for the mental benefits than physical, but damned if I don't manage to get my hands under my butt, then gradually pull one leg at a time through my handcuffed wrists. I move slowly, so slowly that not even a rustle of silk gives away what I'm doing in that back seat. The cop never glances back. It's so easy, I wonder if flexibility isn't another vampire physiological anomaly.

I scoot over so that I'm sitting in the corner, close to the door. "So, how many vampire notches do you have on your gun belt?"

He doesn't answer.

I'm going to bet it's not many or I wouldn't have been able to do what I just did. I almost wish this mind thing worked with humans so I could get inside his head and tell him what a stupid asshole he really is. I'm going to enjoy springing myself on him, seeing the shocked look in those baby blues as I—

My thoughts are cut short as we take the turnoff to Torrey Pines State Park. The cop cruises by the gate with a two-finger salute to the ranger on duty. I almost yell out, knowing the dark tint of the windows in the back of the cruiser prevents the ranger from seeing that this cop is taking a civilian into the park. Not an everyday occurrence, I would think. But the cop doesn't slow down and the opportunity is gone before I can.

Just another thing I'll have to thank this idiot for when I get out of here. I wonder what a cop's blood tastes like—

Wait a minute. What am I doing? I'm just going to get away. I'm not going to linger for a midnight snack, even though he certainly deserves a little bite.

The car pulls deeper into the park. We're off the main road and through the campground, winding through the sparse forest of spectral shapes known as the Torrey Pines. These trees are frozen in perpetual static motion, bent as though buffeted by ghostly sea winds, even on a still night. It's a dark, creepy place and a feeling of foreboding settles in my bones. I've never been this far into the forest, but I hear the ocean pounding somewhere far below and know we must be coming to the end of the road. My recollection of a map of the park showed it dead-ending at the cliffs. This would certainly be a private enough spot to perform whatever ghastly ritual this guy has in mind.

I sit up straighter in the seat, prepare myself for the getaway. The best time to make a run for it will be the

minute he opens the door, before he has time to register
the fact that I have the use of my hands. I will throw my
weight on the door as soon as I hear the lock release and
push it hard enough to make him lose his balance: Then
I'll beat it into the trees. I remember how fast Donaldson
and Avery were. I can only hope that's a hereditary trait
among vampires.

I compose myself. I'm immortal now, according to
Avery. Kin to Lestat, and Count Dracula. Hell, maybe
even a cousin of Spike—my favorite vampire character.
And he's cute, too, to boot. Buffy never treated him
right. Maybe it's not an act with James Marsters. Look
at those cheekbones. Maybe he really is—

You're not taking this very seriously.

The voice is so unexpected, I literally jump in the seat.
"What?" I squeak before I realize that I've spoken out
loud.

My eyes spring to the cop, but if he heard me, he
isn't acting like it. His eyes are still on the road.

Avery?

*No, not Avery. And I said, you're not taking this very
seriously. What's the matter with you?*

The tone is offensive. *I have a short attention span*, I
shoot back. *It's been a problem my whole life.*

*Well, if you don't pull yourself together, it won't be a
problem much longer.*

My head is reeling with this new intrusion into my
thoughts. My eyes find the mirror. It's not the cop. He's
staring straight ahead. Besides, what sense would that
make?

I try to probe, but nothing comes through. *Who are you?*

Not important. What is important is that you get your wits about you. This guy will not be alone. They never are.

Where are you? Are you here to help?

I'm not close enough to be of physical aid. You're going to have to do this on your own. Do you have a plan?

I tell him what I've come up with.

It might work. But you'll have to act quickly, and once you're free, run like hell. Don't look back. I'll be waiting for you on the road outside the park entrance.

How will I know who you are?

I'll be driving your car.

What? That's a ninety thousand dollar automobile. You'd better not—

But the car is slowing and I'm jerked out of my dim-witted retort. I must be crazy, worrying about my car when there's a bunch of lunatics waiting to make sure I never drive the damned thing again.

He's right, I scold myself. Pull yourself together.

It's a good thing I do. The unfamiliar voice in my brain warned me that the cop would not be acting alone. He is right about that, too. There are three figures outlined in the car headlights as we approach. One is holding a burning torch.

Is that how they plan to kill me?

Adrenaline and rage turn my blood to fire. I watch the cop's face as he stops the car and turns in the seat to look at me. Surprise flashes, replaced by a smug contempt.

"Well, you've been busy, haven't you? But no matter. We're about to have a little bonfire. It's chilly out there, but I'm sure you'll be warm enough."

He's stalling while his pals advance on the car. Two on the left, one on the right. A little hint of fear replaces some of the anger churning my stomach. Can I take two of these guys at once? I hadn't planned on a welcoming party.

Your strength, the voice reassures me. *Use your strength.*

All at once, I know. Instead of waiting for them to get to the car, I turn. I brace myself against the front seat and kick at the back window as hard as I can.

Nothing.

I hear the cop yelling in my ear. He can't reach me through the wire partition. I kick out again, this time willing every ounce of strength into my legs. With a sharp crack, the window pops out. I see from the corner of my eye the two men on my left. One of them is shouting and fumbling at the door.

But I'm already vaulting out the back window, scooting over the trunk, scrambling toward the trees. I feel a rush of air and hear angry voices behind me.

Then I'm running, flying over and through the forest.

The voice said not to look back. That's no problem. I'm too afraid to look back.

CHAPTER 15

BLOOD POUNDS IN MY EARS. ADRENALINE-laced fear propels me forward.

It's the most exhilarating thing I've ever experienced.

I've never been much of a runner, but I feel like a gazelle, sure-footed and nimble and headed in the direction of the highway with nothing but instinct to guide me. Suddenly, I'm not winded or afraid. After a moment, the yelling behind me fades. I've beaten all four of them. I've never felt so alive.

Ironic.

Somewhere along the way, I've broken the cuffs apart. I think it happened when I reached up to brush a low-hanging branch away from my face. One moment my wrists were bound together and the next, my hands were free. It happened with no conscious effort on my part.

All this time, I thought I needed the key when all I really needed was to pull hard enough.

I'm approaching the road now, so I allow myself to slow down. I'm not sure where Casper, my friendly voice, is going to be. I send out the question, but get no response.

The sound of traffic is louder now, and I veer away from the park entrance. I don't know how long it will take the four stooges to drive back this way, but I take no chances. I stay in the tree line and out of sight. It's a climb up to the highway from here, but I bound up the steep incline with no effort.

I work my way through the thinning trees until I have a line of sight to the road. Cautiously scanning both directions, I spy my car about a quarter mile away, on this side of the highway, facing south. I wait only a heartbeat to see if there are headlights coming behind me, along the park road. When I'm sure there are none, I race across the open shoulder to the car.

Thank you, thank you, thank you, I sing as I pull open the car door.

There's no one inside.

The keys are in the ignition, the engine is running. But there is no one inside. I'm disappointed, but I don't waste any time indulging it. I slip into the driver's seat, put the Jag in gear and pull out. There'll be time later to track down my new guardian angel.

Now the question becomes where to go? These guys obviously know about me, making me wonder if it's safe to go home. On the other hand, maybe it's Avery they're watching, and anyone coming out of his compound is suspect. Could be why the cop dragged me out of the car. He saw no reflection in the car window and knew.

There's only one way to find out.

On the way back to Avery's, I keep checking the rearview mirror to see if I'm being followed. I debate whether I should have gone home to change cars, but when I pull up to his driveway, I'm pretty sure I'm alone.

The drive has taken far less time this early in the morning. I'm at the gated entrance in minutes. I don't expect the gate to be standing open, but it is, so I go on up to the house. The driveway is empty, all of Avery's guests departed. I grab my purse and head for the door.

Like before, Avery answers the bell himself. He's dressed in the same slacks, but this time, they're topped with a red silk robe and he has doe skin slippers on his feet. He's got a book in one hand and a martini glass in the other.

I don't wait to be invited in but breeze by with an airy wave of my hand.

"Nice look, Avery. Very Hugh Heffner."

He stops me by hooking a finger in one of the cuffs dangling like a clunky charm bracelet from my wrist and holding it up. "Nice look, Anna. Very Courtney Love."

He's not surprised to see me—it doesn't come through in his expression or his thoughts. In fact, he smiles and points the martini glass in my direction.

I didn't expect you back so soon. Would you like a drink?

So soon? I nod and follow him into the library, working at the cuffs with the key from my purse until they open and fall free. I toss the broken cuffs onto the desk. There's a fire going in here now, and after pouring me a glass from a chilled decanter on the desk and adding a tiny skewer, we take seats in front of it.

But you did expect me back.

He has the good grace not to feign ignorance. He points the glass at my wrists in a mock salute.

I heard about what happened tonight. I was not surprised at the outcome. I told you your powers are growing. Maybe now you'll believe it.

I take a sip of the martini—gin, very dry, with two olives and a cocktail onion. Just the way I like it.

"You *were* expecting me."

Avery shrugs. "Not expecting, exactly. I thought you might have questions after your ordeal."

I look at him over the rim of my glass. "How did you find out about it so soon?"

"I told you, you're being watched."

I take another taste of the martini. *Did you set it up?*

That seems to surprise him. His thoughts shut down for the length of two heartbeats, then open to me again.

No. But I thought we cleared that up earlier. If I meant to harm you, I would have done it earlier. In the hospital or at your house, when we were alone.

Did you send someone to my aid? The person watching me, perhaps?

This time, the surprise is genuine.

What do you mean?

I debate not telling him. Perhaps I should keep Casper

to myself. But I don't shut off quickly enough. He reads what happened before I can prevent it.

He draws a quick, sharp breath. Interesting. *Seems you have a second protector.*

Are you telling me you don't know who it was?

He shakes his head.

But I thought you knew everybody.

This brings a smile. *No, Anna, I don't know everybody.*

So, just how many vampires are there in San Diego?

You mean in the City of San Diego or the entire county?

I blow out a burst of air. *Let's start with the city.*

Avery purses his lips and begins running a list of names through his head.

I stop him when he gets to twenty. I can't keep the astonishment out of my voice. "How could this not be general knowledge? How do you manage to keep your existence a secret with that many high profile vampires running around?"

He arches a brow. "You mean *our* existence. It's taken centuries of being hunted down like animals to make us realize secrecy is our only weapon against the kind of murderous bigotry you experienced tonight. It's also the reason I told you we have to stop Donaldson. His killings are already attracting too much attention. The fact that you were picked up so soon confirms it. Perhaps they—"

But I'm not interested in Avery's ramblings. I interrupt his train of thought with my own.

I want to know who they are.

Avery picks up the thread and smoothly switches mental gears. *They call themselves "Revengers."*

I sniff. Cute. *I suppose, like the Night Watchers, there's a story behind the name.*

Avery nods. *The Revengers came into existence during the Middle Ages. The first group was formed to avenge the deaths of three crusaders killed by vampires during a particularly bloody attempt to convert some unwilling townspeople to Christianity. No matter that the crusaders had already pillaged the town and put every man and boy to the sword. It was the vampires stopping them that attracted the ire of the church. They sent a small army out to hunt them down and kill them. And they made the townspeople accomplices, though up to that time vampires lived in peace with mortals.*

I raise an eyebrow. *I thought we were always the bad guys. You know, harvesting men to feed the hunger.*

Avery shakes his head. *No. In fact, vampires were often protectors of a town. Night Watchers, remember?*

The original Night Watchers were vampires?

Who better to patrol the night?

I'm finding this all incredible. "Everything I've ever thought or heard about vampires seems not to be true," I say. "Why all the misconception? Why don't we come out of the closet and clear things up? That would put an end to the Revengers once and for all."

Avery shrugs. "Not possible. For one thing, who would believe us? All we would accomplish is making our individual identities known. We might as well paint a bull's-eye on our backs. Secrecy is our best weapon against those who seek to destroy us."

"Well, your identity is obviously not so secret. I figure they picked me up when I left here."

Avery's brow wrinkles. *Why would you think that?*

I flutter a hand. "Why? Because I was on my way home from here when I got stopped. And the cop wasted no time in getting me into his car. How else would he know I was a vampire?"

"Did he shine a light in your eyes first?"

Now it's my turn to be surprised. *As a matter of fact, he did. It almost blinded me.*

And weren't you speeding when you were stopped?

You got that from reading my thoughts, didn't you?

He smiles a hard, cold-eyed smile. "I told you to be careful, not to call attention to yourself, didn't I? And what's the first thing you do, drive that sports car of yours one hundred miles an hour down a city street. *That's* why you were stopped. And the light is the way they check for us. It's a high-intensity strobe bulb. It affects the vampire physiology. Disorients us. That cop wasn't looking for a vampire when he stopped you. He lucked into finding one, and you made it easy."

I have to grudgingly concede that everything Avery says rings true. Uncertainty creeps into my consciousness. "So now they know about me, don't they?"

Avery shoots me a black, layered look. "And you may have led them right here. To me."

Guilt makes me turn away from Avery. I was so sure I had been picked up leaving here. The possibility that I may, in fact, have put him in danger fills me with dismay. It was a stupid, rookie mistake.

Getting to my feet, I place the glass on a small table between our two chairs. *I'd better go.*

But he's on his feet, too, and he stops me before I reach the door. His hands are on my arms.

You can't go, Anna. It won't be safe for you to return to the cottage. You'd better stay here.

My first reaction is to object—to his hands on me, to the idea that I'm not safe on my own. But his touch sends an involuntary tremor through me. I try, but I can't hide the reaction. I'm suddenly flooded with the memory of how it felt when I was drinking his blood. I find myself wondering how the rest would be.

"You can find out."

He takes a step closer, heat and desire radiating from his skin. I feel his lips, a feather touch at the hollow of my throat, tantalizing, persuasive. I close my eyes and sway into him. His lips part. His breath burns.

I'm lost.

He lowers my body to the floor. His hands are gentle and sure as they gather my skirt up around my waist, unbutton my blouse, and pull it all free. His robe falls open, exposing a smooth, bare chest. I fumble with his belt, unzip his pants. He yanks them off and presses himself against me. His skin is cool beneath my fingertips, but there's heat where our bodies touch. Electricity arcs between us, and gusts of desire that shake my very being.

Then he's inside me, and I'm inside him, passion making us one. When his blood fills my mouth, and mine his, the raw act of mutual possession is complete.

I abandon myself to a whirl of sensation, the pleasure pure and explosive.

Nothing that has come before prepares me for this. I'm dreadfully afraid that nothing will ever be the same.

CHAPTER 16

I'M GLAD WHEN I AWAKEN IN AVERY'S BIG BED that I am alone. I pull myself into a sitting position from a tangle of silk sheets and look around. Sunlight from huge, arched windows illuminates a room filled with antiques—heavy, carved, and made of some rich, exotic wood.

No dark, dank casket filled with earth from the motherland for this vampire.

Still, I hold my head in my hands and groan.

What have I done?

On the nightstand, there's a decanter of coffee and a china cup, along with a single red rose in a crystal vase and a note that simply says, "You were wonderful." I feel as if I'm living a scene from a bad romance novel.

I groan again. The night is a blur in my mind, but I

remember that there was sex—a lot of it—and the taste of blood as intoxicating as any wine.

You were wonderful.

No, it's not a romance novel, it's a bad fantasy novel complete with a rakish vampire and his eager protégé.

I finger the note. *Very* eager protégé, evidently.

I put a tentative hand to my neck, but there's nothing to feel. No puncture marks, no raised skin. Did I remember to do the same for Avery?

I swing my legs out of bed. *That* I feel. I'm sore and chafed, and as I stumble off to find the bathroom, I wonder if Avery is having the same trouble.

The thought that he might be a little tender today, too, brings a smile to my lips.

Where are my clothes?

I get the answer when I swing open the bathroom door. My clothes have been neatly hung on a hanger, my panties and bra folded on the edge of the tub. It's a big tub, with jacuzzi jets and a lot of decorative bottles promising perfumed delights.

I succumb.

I'm soaking in a jasmine-scented whirlpool when the first dose of reality hits.

Max.

What *have* I done?

I sink deeper into the water.

I was protecting Max, wasn't I? From myself. And it's not like we're married or engaged or anything.

Right.

Well, we've never even talked about it. We've just had—what?

What have Max and I had?

I lay my head back on the cool tile. I'm already thinking of him in the past tense.

The reality brings a wave of sadness. I love Max. I think. We've been together for almost two years—well, as together as a couple can be when one of them is an undercover drug enforcement agent. It's the first long-term relationship I've had in years, and it's built on mutual respect and trust.

At least it was.

Trust.

I trust Max, and Max trusts me.

Would he trust me now, if he knew about Avery?

About Avery? Hell, what if he knew about me?

I'm a vampire, for chrissake. A vampire.

"And a very beautiful one, I might add."

Avery's voice startles me into sitting straight up in the water. I jump so high, water splashes over the side and onto the floor in a mini-riptide. I turn and glare at him.

Don't do that. Don't sneak up on me.

He laughs and moves toward me, stripping off a tie and shirt as he comes.

I knew there was a reason I had that tub installed.

He steps out of slacks and boxers and stands naked, looking down at me.

I reach out, smiling, and caress a muscular thigh.

"Aren't you going to invite me in?" he says at last.

But I don't answer; my mouth is otherwise engaged.

LATER, BACK IN THE BEDROOM, I STRETCH AND yawn and look over at Avery. *Don't you have to go to the hospital?*

Avery is leaning back against the headboard, his arm around me, sipping coffee from that elegant china cup.

I went in while you were asleep. Checked on a few patients, cleared the rest of my schedule. I thought you and I might spend the day together.

Avery, I can't spend all day here. I have to get home. I just wonder if there will be a welcoming party waiting for me.

Avery sits up straighter. *I've been thinking about that cop who picked you up last night. You know, he may not have run your license plate. He wouldn't want it on record that he stopped you, particularly if you suddenly disappeared. Unless he wrote your license number down somewhere, he might not be able to trace you. I'll call Captain Williams later and see what he can find out. You didn't get a badge number or name or anything, did you?*

I shake my head. *I wish I'd thought of it. Everything happened too fast.*

Well, just don't drive that Jag for a while.

I roll toward him. "Why don't you come home with me? We can take a walk on the beach. I can show you some of my favorite haunts."

He doesn't answer, but what he's thinking comes through loud and clear—too loud and clear. It's a good thing I can read what he's feeling as well as his thoughts. He feigns horror as he contemplates dingy, smoke-filled dives with sawdust-strewn floors populated by hygiene-challenged, shaggy-haired surfers.

"Very funny," I comment. "You've been breathing this rarified air too long." *Oops, wait a minute—we don't breathe air anymore, do we?*

There's a sardonic twist to that sexy mouth.

"After what happened in that bathtub," he says, "you have to ask?"

IT'S NOON WHEN I HAUL MYSELF OUT TO MY CAR and gingerly climb inside. It's been the most bizarre twenty-four hours of my life. I've been kidnapped by the police and had sex with a three-hundred-year-old vampire, during which I actually drank his blood and enjoyed it. More than enjoyed it.

All of it.

I turn the Jag toward home. Avery wanted me to wait for him, to leave my car there, but I'm anxious to get back. I told him I'd put the car right into the garage where it won't be seen. I want to shower and change clothes and check in with David. He's probably called about a dozen times and will be frantic because he couldn't reach me.

David is like that.

And it's time we get back to work. I'm sure Jerry will have jobs lined up, and I need something other than this new "nature" of mine to think about.

I reach for my purse and shake loose my cell phone.

David's number is on speed dial, and I punch it before I remember he's in L.A. with Gloria.

I'm just about to disconnect when he answers with an abrupt, "Jesus, Anna. Where have you been?"

"David? You're back home?"

"Never mind that. Where are you?"

"I'm on my way to the beach. Why?"

"Get here as fast as you can." He said *here*.

"You're at the cottage?"

There's a brief pause. "What's left of it." His voice softens. "There's been a fire."

CHAPTER 17

A FIRE?
I drop the phone and concentrate on driving. I've just passed Grand Avenue when I see the smoke. Panic twists my stomach. I'm a half mile away, but I can't get closer because fire equipment blocks Mission. I leave the car in the parking lot of a 7-Eleven and start running.

I see David first, standing with a group of firemen. Only the firemen aren't holding hoses or wielding pick axes. In fact, they aren't doing anything at all except standing around chatting with my ex-football player partner.

It makes me angry. Why aren't they fighting the fire? I open my mouth to yell, but something stops me.

I look down the street, toward the cottage.

I know now why the firemen are clustered in their little circle, with David holding court. He may as well.

There's nothing left of my home except smoldering debris.

I stop short, heart hammering so hard I think it will burst my chest.

Nothing left.

I feel someone touch my arm.

"Anna."

It's David.

But I turn away from him and walk toward the burned out shell that used to be my grandmother's cottage. I hear him call out to me, but I don't stop and I don't turn around. I can't.

There are two firemen picking through the rubble. One of them notices me and comes over. He's young, but his eyes are somber, and his voice full of compassion when he asks, "Was this your home, ma'am?"

I nod, unable to tear my eyes away from his partner. He's moving through the debris, dousing little tongues of fire that lap to the surface here and there as the air hits.

"Is there anything left?"

He shakes his head. "Won't be able to tell for a day or so. You'll have to wait until things cool off and our investigation is complete before you can go in. There'll be security posted, to protect the integrity of the scene. Offhand, though, I'd say it's pretty much a total loss. I'm sorry."

A total loss.

David is at my side again. This time, he opens his arms and gathers me against his chest. I let him, though

I don't have the strength to raise my own arms and hug back. I can only stand there, eyes on the ruins.

Finally, he pulls back and looks down at me. There's a flash of surprise, and I know it's registering that all traces of my wounds are gone. He doesn't comment on it, though. Instead, he makes a gesture toward the uniformed policeman approaching us from the sidewalk. "They have some questions for you."

I nod and let the policeman lead me over to his car. He's middle-aged and paunchy, with a kind face and sad eyes. He must think I look shaky, because he opens the passenger door and motions for me to sit.

I do, sliding in sideways. He leans down and begins to ask questions. I answer the best I can, though shock is taking its toll.

No, I was not home last night.

No, I'd rather not give the name of my companion if it's not necessary at this time.

No, I don't know why anyone would do this.

Yes, I have insurance.

The interview drags on until another policeman approaches. He touches the arm of the cop interviewing me, and they both move to the side, out of my hearing. In a moment, they are back—thanking me for my time, assuring me that they will be in touch.

David draws near, offering me a hand out of the car. Like an automaton, I push myself off the seat.

"How could this happen? I don't understand," I say.

He shakes his head. "I don't either. The fire chief thinks this was no accident. They've already started an investigation. They can pinpoint the origin of the fire, and it seems to be dead center in the cottage. They've found traces of an accelerant."

He pauses, an uncomfortable silence stretching between us as I see him bristling with a question he's suddenly afraid of or unsure how to ask. His hands clasp and unclasp at his side.

"What is it?"

David lets out a breath in a noisy rush. "Where have you been, Anna? I've been trying to call you all night. Do you have any idea how worried I was? Your cell phone was turned off, you didn't answer at the cottage. And don't try telling me you were with Michael. He told me he hadn't heard from you for a month—"

"Jesus, David. You didn't say anything to him about what happened, did you?"

"No," he snaps right back. "But I should have. You lied to me about calling him. I don't understand what's going on with you. And now this. Do you realize how scared I was when I got here and saw the fire? I didn't know if you were alive or dead."

Alive or dead. That comment brings a bitter smile to the corners of my mouth. I can't help it. The irony of his statement is lost on him, of course.

I close my eyes and fight back the panic. David rages on.

"What's the matter with you? Are you in shock? Is that why you're acting so crazy? I told Dr. Avery you shouldn't have been released from the hospital. It was too soon. After everything that happened, he should have kept you there longer. I should have insisted. Or I should have stayed here with you."

He looks and sounds as if he's just getting started, but I can't take any more. I take a step back and hold up a hand. "This isn't helping, David. I'm sorry you were worried. I'm sorry I didn't call. I can't explain it. I don't want to. All I have energy for now is seeing if there's anything left of my life to salvage."

His face reddens, though I can't tell if it's because he's embarrassed or still angry. Suddenly, weariness washes over his features and I'm instantly ashamed of my outburst. He's been my friend and partner for two and a half years and I haven't even asked him how he's feeling. Of course, *his* house hasn't just burned to the ground. Still, in all the trauma of the last two days, I'd completely forgotten that David was involved, too.

I take a tiny step toward him. "I didn't call you because I thought you'd be spending time with Gloria. I didn't mean for you to worry."

His expression shifts again, lines hardening around his mouth. "Turns out she had a modeling job in New York. She figured if she got me to L.A., she could talk me into accompanying her. I told her I couldn't leave you—not with all that's happened."

He pauses, confusion softening the lines on his face. "But look at you, Anna. Two nights ago you were attacked by a psycho, yet here you are this morning, not a scratch on you and dressed as if you just came from a party. Your house is burning to the ground right in front of you, and so far, I haven't seen a glimmer of emotion."

I don't know how to respond to that. It doesn't matter, though, because he just keeps talking.

"I know what the problem is, Anna. It's that damned Dr. Avery. He let you leave the hospital before you were ready. You're still in shock and that quack should have known it, but did he care? I'm going to find Dr. Avery and when I do—"

I put a gentle hand on David's arm to stop the tirade. "It's not Dr. Avery's fault my house burned. And you may not want to hear this, but you're wrong about him. He's been—" I suddenly find myself groping for the right words. "Well, he's kind of taken care of me the last day or so."

"What?" The lines around his mouth become pronounced again as it twists into an exasperated frown. "He's been in touch with you?"

He's definitely been in touch with me. I nod.

"I can't believe his nerve. What was he doing? Covering his ass? He must know he made a mistake letting you leave the hospital. He's not going to get away with this. This is malpractice at the very least. Anna, we're going to sue the hospital."

Now I'm the one suddenly overcome with weariness. I don't want to fight with him anymore, and I don't want to defend Avery or myself. I turn away from David and walk back toward what's left of my home.

One of my neighbors, a dentist with the gaudiest house on the block, calls my name, holding something out to me over the police barricade.

"Anna," he says. "What a mess, huh? Lucky the firemen got here so fast. I saw the smoke and called them, then got to work with a garden hose. Saved my house. Sorry they couldn't save yours. But take this. It's my architect's business card. He'll get you a place built in no time."

A place like his? It's beyond horrible. Still, I take the card and ball it into my fist. Maybe the guy is capable of building something other than the pink stucco monstrosity next door. I do have to think about that—

Another flash of movement and a voice in my head. *Anna, what's happening?*

I turn to see Avery coming across the street. I'd forgotten he was going to join me here. Unfortunately, David sees him, too. I'm not quick enough to warn Avery off and he runs smack into David.

David puts out a hand and shoves Avery back. "Don't go near her," he says. "I'm warning you. You've done enough damage."

I feel Avery tense, see the danger flash in his eyes.

Don't hurt him, Avery, I say. *Please. Go on home. I'll catch up with you later.*

Avery's eyes never leave David's face. He is standing so still, so utterly motionless, I fear he has shut me out. An almost primordial rage blazes out from him. While we were in the hospital, Avery put up with David. Here, he doesn't seem so inclined.

I try again. *Avery. Please. He's my friend and he's worried about me. Let it go.*

A long moment passes. Avery's eyes shift to meet mine. I feel his anger ease off, see the set of his shoulders relax. *For you,* he tells me. *But your partner needs to learn respect.*

He takes a step backward from David, and in that moment, I get to them. I put a hand on David's arm. "It's all right, David. Let Dr. Avery go. He just came to check up on me. He'll leave now."

The last was as much for Avery as for David. He bends his head in a single nod and steps away. *Will you come to me later?* he asks.

I will. I have to finish here first.

Avery says nothing to David, and simply turns on his heel and heads back in the direction he came. I know David has turned to me and is saying something but another voice, or rather, impression has interposed itself in my consciousness. It's there, nebulous and tentative, but as nerve jangling as a jolt of electricity.

I look around quickly to see where or who it's coming from, being careful to keep my own thoughts from projecting outward. Someone is reaching out to probe my mind. Is it my anonymous friend from last night?

I scan the crowd until I recognize a face. It appears for only a brief moment, and then it is swallowed up by the milling group of curiosity seekers gathered across the street.

It's only a glimpse, but I know. I feel it in my very bones.

Donaldson is here.

CHAPTER 18

FOR AN INSTANT, THE FIRE, DAVID, EVERYTHING else fades from my consciousness. Only Donaldson's presence burns through. Avery said Donaldson and I have a connection. Is this what he meant? Does Avery pick up on it, too?

But in a flash, I no longer sense Donaldson. He's simply there one moment and gone the next. I don't know how this vampire radar works. Can I call out to Avery without Donaldson picking up on it? If I can get Avery to follow Donaldson, maybe together we can make him talk, find out if he's behind the fire and why.

When Donaldson doesn't "reappear" for several minutes, and I don't spot him in the crowd, I take the chance.

Avery, are you near?

There's no response.

Avery?

Still nothing.

And David is now actually shaking my arm, trying to get my attention.

"Anna. Anna, what's wrong?"

Reluctantly, I drag my thoughts back from the ether and concentrate on my friend. "I'm all right."

But David shakes his head. "You're not all right. God damn that Avery. I should—"

"David, enough. If you really want to know what's wrong I'll tell you. I can't take you ragging Avery's ass all the time. He's a good doctor and he's as concerned about me as you are. Just let it go."

I'm not sure if it's my tone or the fact that I'm sticking up for Avery, but it's obvious that I've gone too far. Hurt and disappointment darken David's eyes. He stiffens and pulls away. "Well, I'm sorry I offended your new friend. I'll try to be nicer next time."

He's angry with me. I just don't know what to do about it. Obviously, I can't tell him I won't be seeing Avery anymore—or maybe that's exactly what I should tell him. It's a lie, of course, but I have a feeling I'll be telling a lot of lies from now on. Might as well get this one over with.

I put my hand on his arm. "David, listen to me. There won't be a next time. This was Avery's last visit. He's gone now, and you can forget about him."

It takes a minute for that to penetrate. David looks down at me with a puzzled scowl, and then his frown lines begin to relax and jaw muscles to unclench. "Is that true? This is the last time you're going to see him?"

"That's what I said."

"Good. That's good."

Someone calls out to me from the cluster of fire and police personnel beginning their mop-up. It's a way to end this conversation, so I leave David to join them. They hand me forms and business cards and the patrolman who questioned me asks for a number where I can be reached. I give them my cell since I don't know for sure where I'll be. I suspect it will be Avery's, but I don't have his number. That piece of paper is just another ash among the sea of ashes that used to be my house.

"Give him my number." David's voice at my elbow makes me jump. "You can stay with me."

God, here we go again.

I flash back to the scene in the hospital, but this time, Gloria is not in the picture. I can't use her as an excuse to refuse. I'm not up to another argument with David so I just agree. "Sure. That's a good idea, David. Thanks."

The officer takes his number and address and wraps things up. The two firemen still working the debris remain, but everyone else climbs into various emergency vehicles and soon the street is open once again. David tugs gently on my elbow, and I follow him to his car. All the rancor he directed toward Avery and me seems to have dissipated like dust in the wind.

He opens the passenger door, but I decline with a shake of my head.

"It will be better if I follow you. I want to go to my folks first. I can borrow some clothes to tide me over until I have time to shop. I'll pack a bag and come over later, okay?"

For once, he doesn't argue. He just asks, "Do you want me to go with you?"

I give him a grateful little peck on the cheek. "No, but thanks. I think I need a few minutes alone after all this."

Of course, what I'm thinking is that I'll head straight for Avery's. But since David doesn't have a clue about that, he acquiesces gracefully. I watch as he pulls away, and then I head back down the block for my car. It's still sitting in the store parking lot, but there's a silver BMW parked alongside. I don't pay much attention until I realize there's someone sitting inside watching my approach.

Avery?

He leans across and opens the passenger side door so I can slip inside. *How are you?*

With that simple question, something breaks deep inside me. Tears I can't control run down my face. Then I'm in Avery's arms, and before I can stop, I'm sobbing against his chest. All the incredible, frightening, puzzling things that have happened to me in the last few days pale into insignificance at the realization that I've just lost what I held most dear. My grandmother's wonderful legacy, all her memories, were a part of that house.

They're gone now and it's my fault.

Avery is stroking my hair. *Why do you think that? This was an accident. You can't blame yourself.*

He doesn't know what the fireman told me. I let him pick through the recollection of our conversation. *And Donaldson was there, too*, I add after a moment.

Donaldson?

I saw him, and I tried to signal you, but you didn't answer.

Avery pulls a handkerchief from his pocket and holds it out to me. *Too much interference out here, I guess. Those damned microwave towers for cell phones are everywhere. I'm sorry. Do you think he started the fire?*

I'm sitting up straighter in the seat now, wiping my face with the handkerchief. *I don't know. I can't figure out why he would. Unless he thought I was inside and he was trying to kill me.*

But even as I say this, David's words come back to me. "No," I amend with a shake of my head. "The fire chief said the fire started in the middle of the cottage. If he was inside, he knew I wasn't there."

I look into Avery's eyes. "I felt him, just like you said I would. He was there for an instant, and then he was gone."

Avery's brow creases and his mouth grows tight and grim. He is shielding his thoughts, but I sense his disquiet. Finally, he says, "You must stay with me until we can sort this out."

I blow out an exasperated breath and let my thoughts answer.

I can't. David is extremely upset with you—and with me. I told him I wouldn't see you again. Of course, it was a lie. But I need to stay with him at least tonight. After that, I'll tell him I'm going to stay at my parents' home. He knows they're in Europe for two weeks. He'll accept that.

David is a mortal. Avery's tone is dismissive. *You*

don't need to explain yourself to him or to anyone ever again. You are vampire, Anna, and you must learn to act like it.

His air of superiority makes me cringe. *If that's true, I remind him gently, why do we hide our true identities?*

He cocks an eyebrow at me. *You are impudent, aren't you? Perhaps it's why I like you so much. You have a way of bringing me back to earth. All right, Anna, maybe it's best if you run along to your friend's. But I want to see you first thing tomorrow morning. I'll check around tonight and see if I can learn where Donaldson is hiding. Perhaps we can find out just what he's up to.*

I start to get out of the car, letting his remark about "running along to my friend" pass without comment. I don't need his permission. But I do need his help.

He reaches out, placing one hand on my arm, cupping my chin in his other hand.

"It will be all right, you know."

His eyes offer solace. For this moment at least, I let myself accept it.

CHAPTER 19

M Y PARENTS LIVE IN LA MESA, A BEDROOM
community east of San Diego. A drive that
should take twenty minutes max, takes about forty with
traffic, but for once, I'm in no hurry. It's the first time
I've been alone—really alone—in days. The crying jag
in Avery's car released some pent-up emotion, but while
the sadness is gone, anger is just bubbling to the surface.

For the first time in my life, I know how it feels to
want someone dead. If Donaldson is behind the fire, I
might just reconsider Avery's notion that he needs to be
killed. I'm not shocked that I feel this way, nor do I
blame it on how I've changed. It has nothing to do with
being vampire and everything to do with what Donaldson has taken from me.

It's a most human reaction.

Which is comforting, in a crazy sort of way.

At my folks, the reality of the fire hits me again. Their home is filled with silver-framed pictures, several of them of my grandparents taken in and around the cottage. I pick up one of them and hug it to my chest as I head for the bedroom.

My mom is a high school principal, my dad an investment banker. I'm an only child. I had a brother, Steve, two years older than me. He died at eighteen in one of the most senseless, devastating ways imaginable. He was struck by a drunk driver in the middle of the day in the middle of a crosswalk on his way to classes at Cornell University.

I don't know what makes me think of Steve now. Maybe it's because here in the house where we grew up, his presence is still felt. Not in a maudlin, there's a shrine on top of the television kind of way. But rather in an affirmation that life does go on after such a tragedy. My parents worked hard to make sure I didn't get lost in the depths of their inconsolable grief.

Which is what makes my parents so crazy about the lifestyle I've chosen. I know this. I just can't tell them why I feel the way I do. I can't explain that it's *because* of Steve's death I live my life as I do. He was killed minding his own business, without warning or reason. If life is so tenuous, I'll be damned if I spend it in safe drudgery.

But that's rather a moot point now, isn't it?

Maybe now, with eternity stretching out in front of me, I could stand to take a normal job if only to appease them in the short time we have left together.

Because I know, it is a short time. Not that they are

in ill health, but because I realize it is only a matter of years before they notice that their daughter is not aging. There will be no wrinkles on my face, no sagging body, no arthritic joints. How will I handle it? Will I have to disappear? How can I bear to watch as they lose another child? There must be another way. I must ask Avery.

Avery. What would I do without him?

The smell of smoke in my hair and on my skin brings me out of my reverie. I slip out of my clothes and head for the bathroom off my folk's bedroom. I let the water run hot before I step into the shower. The steam is a balm to my spirit, as well as my body. I lather up and rinse off, and then I stand there for ten minutes, not thinking, not feeling. When I can stand the heat no longer, I step out.

The bathroom has turned into a steam room. I wrap a towel around my head and grab another to swipe over the mirror. It takes a minute for the glass to clear and another to digest the fact that there is no reflection staring back at me.

The jolt is followed by an awareness that to no longer have to deal with mortal vanity is rather liberating. I towel dry my hair, finger comb it, and I'm done.

It only takes a few minutes more to change into jeans and a tee shirt and throw some clothes into a bag. My mother and I are the same size, and while her taste leans toward the sophisticated, she does have a stash of casual wear that I take advantage of now. I leave her a note telling her what I've taken. She'll have lots of questions, but there's no sense adding anything else. My parents will learn about the fire when they get back from Europe—soon enough.

Then I'm back in the car and heading for David's loft. He lives in the Gaslamp area just south of downtown where gentrification is in full swing. The area, once a hangout for the homeless, now teems with restaurants, bars, loft apartments and trendy boutiques. The homeless are still here, of course, but relegated to the side streets now. Cops on horseback make sure they don't venture out where their presence might distress the new residents.

It's about four in the afternoon when I pull into the underground parking garage at David's. I realize I don't have his card key—another casualty of the fire—so I press the intercom button and wait for him to answer.

He doesn't.

I press again. I know he's there, because I can see his Hummer parked in all its yellow splendor just across the lot.

Still no response.

Aggravation spikes. He wants me to stay with him, so where is he when I need him?

I back carefully up the ramp and park on the street. Grabbing my overnight bag, I look up at the security door, wondering how I'll get inside. I don't have that key, either. But as luck would have it, a woman appears just then, a cute little Lab pup in her arms. I hustle up the steps just as she opens the door. We exchange smiles, and I give the pup the mandatory head scratch before bolting inside.

David lives on the top floor of a twelve-story building. The elevator bumps to a stop, and I'm knocking at the door, calling out as I do. The door gives under my touch and I push it open. Obviously, he left it that way for me. He's probably taking the trash out or something, which explains why he didn't answer before.

David's loft was purchased with football money—a ton of it. The living room is comprised of walls of glass so that the view sweeps in an unobstructed arc north from downtown to the bay. That panorama is the first thing you notice when you step inside and it's simply an automatic reaction to wander to the balcony to take it all in.

So, I just stand there, watching sailboats bob and weave on the bay like frisky colts, waiting for my errant partner to put in an appearance. But my thoughts are not on the view. My emotions have once again shifted into overdrive. One moment I'm overcome by sadness at the enormity of my loss, and the next, bathed in cold fury at the thought that it was done deliberately.

Finally, I find myself glancing at my watch. I realize I've been here fifteen minutes, and still there's no David.

Something is wrong.

I step back inside and listen. The loft is eerily quiet. In fact, the stereo David *always* leaves on has been turned off. I take a turn around the place, peeking into bedrooms, baths, the kitchen, and dining room, finally back to the living room.

He's not here.

Which doesn't make sense. If he decided to go to the store or to run a last-minute errand, he would have left me a note. And he certainly wouldn't have left the front door open.

I head back through the dining room, thinking I'll use the kitchen phone to try his cell, when I see them.

David's wallet, car keys and money clip are sitting on the bar in the dining room.

How could I have missed that before?

Something's definitely wrong.

I take a step closer and see something else.

My new vampire senses spring into alert.

There's a smear, dark and viscous, on the corner of the glass table, and another on the rug just below it.

It's blood. I *feel* it.

And just as certainly, I know it is David's blood.

CHAPTER 20

A DREADFUL CONVICTION BUILDS IN MY CHEST.
Somehow, whatever happened to David happened
because of me.

I can't explain why I feel this way. I just know it's
true, the same way I know I'm staring at a smear of
David's blood.

I try to reason it through. There could be another explanation. David may have met with some kind of nasty
accident. I snatch up my cell and call Avery, telling him
what I've found and asking him if he'll check the hospitals close to downtown just in case.

He says he'll do it right away and to meet him at his
house, so I take David's keys from the sideboard and
race back to my car. All the way to La Jolla, my mind
reels with the possibility that I've brought about another
disaster, this time to my very best friend, as a direct result of my new "gift."

Gift. First the fire, then David. Christ, where do I go to return such a gift?

"I don't even want my money back," I shout to the heavens. "Just make my life the way it was before."

But then you wouldn't have the chance to know me, would you?

First there's the shock of recognition. Then impatience. *Why, it's Casper. Back out of the blue.*

The voice sounds amused. *Casper?*

Forget it. I doubt you'd understand. Where are you?

Look in the rearview mirror.

There's a beat-up old pickup behind me. I can't see who's driving through the glare of the sun on the windshield.

What do you want?

A thank you would be nice. I did bring your car to you the other night.

Thank you. Now forgive me if I don't stop to chat. I'm a little preoccupied.

I know. Your friend has been taken.

That almost provokes me into slamming on the brakes. I know I can move fast enough to grab him before he—

Don't try it. I'm older than you. By about one hundred and forty years. Trust me, I'm faster.

I grip the wheel in frustration. *If you know something that can help David and you don't tell me, I don't care how much older you are. I'll hunt you down and kill you.*

I know you will. I don't know who has him. That's the truth.

Then what good are you? Why are you here?

To tell you to be careful. You're going through many changes right now. You haven't had the time to adjust the way you should. Things are skewed. Your instincts may be off.

Is that supposed to help?

It's the best I can do.

Then thanks for nothing. There's no answer, and when I check the rearview mirror, the truck is gone.

AVERY IS WAITING FOR ME AT HIS FRONT DOOR when I pull up. He shakes his head and ushers me inside with a hand on the small of my back.

"He's not in any of the local hospitals. And Chief Williams checked for accident reports, too. None involving David. I'm sorry, Anna."

My anger is quickly becoming scalding fury.

"It's Donaldson, isn't it? He took David to have some kind of leverage on me. But why? What does he want?"

Again, the shake of the head. "I can't answer that. Donaldson is an unknown quantity. If you're right about his starting the fire, though, I think it's a safe bet he wants you out of the way. I suppose it makes sense, in a twisted sort of way. You are his only victim who survived. He may perceive you as a threat."

I start to pace, stomach and mind churning. *He must have known I would go back to the cottage. Why didn't he wait for me there? Why start the fire? Why take David?*

Avery doesn't answer. He doesn't know. I read it in his thoughts. He feels as helpless as I do. Worse. There's hopelessness there, too.

Don't do that, I scold. *David has to be all right. I'll find him. If Donaldson thinks taking him is a way to get to me, he's right.*

What are you going to do?

That elicits a frown. *I don't know. You know the vampire community. Is there a place where a rogue would go to seek refuge?*

Avery probes his mind, considering and rejecting several possibilities, until one surfaces that makes him pause. *Yes, I think I do, though this may be a long shot. But didn't you and David think he was on his way to Mexico when you caught up with him?*

I nod. *His wife found a note he'd written to his girlfriend. He'd made arrangements with somebody across the border to put him up for a while. She gave the note to the police, but there wasn't enough information to track him down.*

Avery smiles, as if I've confirmed his suspicion. He crosses to the library with me following closely in his wake, reaches for an atlas and thumbs it open.

He jabs a finger at the page. *He may be here. Right across the border. The badlands. There's a village that's become a hideout for desperados, both human and vampire. Even the* Federales *fear patrolling there. It's called* Beso de la Muerte *by the locals.*

I sift that through my limited knowledge of Spanish. *Kiss of Death?*

He nods, pointing to a place halfway between Tijuana and Mexicali.

There's nothing out there, I protest. *Just desert.*

Not exactly. There's a ghost town—or at least that's what it looks like to outsiders. Ramshackle buildings and an abandoned mineshaft. But in the mine, there exists an underground community of misfits who live like moles in the tunnels. Their leader is an outlaw called Culebra—it means rattlesnake.

Rattlesnake. Charming. And they live in the tunnels?

Avery nods again. *They have supplies brought in on an abandoned railroad spur. It's all funded by one of Mexico's biggest drug dealers. He provides the goods in return for the occasional use of the place.*

You mean, like a hideout?

More like a dumpsite. When he sends someone there, they generally don't come back.

So, how does Donaldson fit into this delightful scenario?

Avery keeps his thoughts deceptively composed. *I'm not sure he does, of course, but it seems a likely place for him to go.*

Of course it does. A hideout like that would be the perfect place for Donaldson, especially if he's after me. I'd follow him, and he could dispose of me—and David—and no one would be the wiser.

I look up at Avery. "It's what you're afraid of, isn't it?"

It's what you should be afraid of, he says. *Donaldson is cunning and cruel. If he's solicited the help of that community, you might not be able to protect yourself.*

What choice do I have? David is more than a business partner; he's a friend.

He's mortal, Anna.

He lets a moment pass, sifting my emotions through his head, feeling my outrage. He holds up a hand as if to ward off the anger I've directed at him.

I'm just saying that you don't have to do this, not really. You could wait for Donaldson to come back here, where you're in your element, and not meet him in his.

And in the meantime, what happens to David?

I pick up his ambivalence, and it notches my fury higher. *I will bring David back. And if this attitude of yours toward mortals is indicative of the vampire community, I don't want to be a part of it.*

You have no choice. His eyes darken. *You are vampire. You don't seem to grasp that. Your realities are no longer founded in the fate of the mortal world. You have a higher calling.*

I feel the rage erupt. *Higher calling? One of my vampire cousins with this higher calling just burned my house down and kidnapped my best friend. Avery, we're blood-sucking freaks. Forgive me if I feel more allegiance to David than to Donaldson—or to you.*

He shakes his head, but there's no acrimony, only a kind of sad resignation. *You don't understand. I appreciate that. This is all so new to you. Trust me, though, when I say that as time goes by, what I'm telling you now will make sense. Donaldson is indeed a freak. And he must be dealt with. But it's because of the damage he is doing to our community, not because of your personal vendetta.*

Is that supposed to make a difference to me?

Maybe not now. But you must learn to separate your feelings for mortals from what is most important. And that is the preservation of your true family.

Enough. I wave a hand. "I'm wasting time. Can you draw me a map to this place?"

Avery locks me in a gaze for a long moment, gauging any chance of reason or logic—his, of course—making a dent in my determination to go after David. He correctly reads that there is none. The silence grows tight with tension until he breaks it with a noisy sigh.

All right. I'll draw you a map. But getting to this place won't be easy. You'll have to take a four-wheel drive vehicle. Do you have one?

I immediately think of David's Hummer. I am listed as co-owner on his registration for business purposes. But that would be too high profile a vehicle to take into Mexico.

I agree, Avery chimes in. *I have an Explorer. You can use that.*

What if the Border patrol asks to see the registration? It's against their laws to take a borrowed vehicle into Mexico.

I'll take care of that. I have friends on the Border Patrol. I'll alert them and they'll see you're not bothered.

Or you could go with me.

Avery smiles. *I wish I could go with you. I would feel much better if I were there to protect you. But I'm a doctor. I have patients who depend on me. I can't just pick up and disappear for a few days.*

"I don't want you to go for protection," I snap angrily.

"I can take care of myself. I want you to go because you know about these things and I don't."

Vampire things, you mean?

Of course. Human vermin I can deal with.

Avery shakes his head. "Well, if you want to wait for a few days—"

Forget it. Just draw the damn map.

Avery doesn't respond to my rancor. He traces a route for me to follow, noting access roads that will lead me to the town. We don't communicate again except for the occasional clarification of a turn-off point or the description of a physical landmark to guide me along the abandoned roadway. When he's done, he reaches inside a desk drawer and pulls out a set of keys.

To the Explorer, he says.

I take the keys and gather up the map. *Anything else you can tell me that might help? Can I transform myself into a wolf or evaporate into a puff of smoke?*

He smiles. *Not yet.*

I turn to go. His voice stops me at the doorway.

Be careful, Anna. I want you back safely.

Thanks, Avery. But it would mean more if you wanted David back, too.

He doesn't reply to that.

CHAPTER 21

THE AFTERNOON SHADOWS ARE LENGTHENING toward sunset when I finally break free of the border bottleneck at Tijuana. I turn east on Highway 2, anxious to get to the cutoff before dark. Avery said it would be hard to find during the day. I imagine it will be almost impossible at night.

The Explorer is brand new, the leather interior still squeaky and aromatic. The car has everything, including an OnStar navigation system. I'm sure that will be of comfort to Avery should I end up in that dumpsite. At least he'll get his car back.

I'm still irritated at his attitude toward David. Hell, toward the whole human race. And he's a doctor, of all things. Does he even see the irony in that?

Shifting in the seat, I turn on the radio. Bright, shrill music fills the cab. It's no comfort. Mexico is not my favorite place. There's the heat, dust, poverty and a ridiculous exchange rate. Not to mention the pollution that periodically closes down the beaches right at my front door. But what am I doing? Why am I thinking about that now?

I pass a hand over my face.

Because it's better than thinking about how scared I am. And it's a way to avoid what's festering in the back of my mind like a raw, open wound.

I don't know what I am or what I'm becoming. I don't know how to handle what's happened with Avery. I don't know where I'll go now that I've lost my home, and I don't know what I'll do if I can't save David.

Not an option. I *will* save David. I have to. It's the only thing I'm really sure of. It's the only hope I have to save myself.

NIGHTTIME HITS THE DESERT WITH A FINALITY missing at the ocean. One minute it's light, the next darkness descends like a window shade being drawn. Even with the car lights, the ambiguous road is not easy to navigate. I know from Avery's map that the access to the town is coming up but the landmark, a lone scrub pine, is swallowed up by the night. There's not even the sliver of a moon to help light the way.

I slow down, unsure how to proceed. The harsh glare of the headlamps doesn't seem to help. Impulsively, I flip them off. Ambient light filters into the cab, and with a start, I realize I can actually see much better. The landscape jumps into stark relief.

Vampire night vision?

God, there's so much to learn.

I search for the pine. It's about half a mile ahead and to the right. There's an arroyo to the left. The perfect place to leave the car. Maneuvering it behind the shield of a clump of scrawny cacti, I jump out and stow the keys under a nearby rock. I don't want them jangling in my pockets.

I've memorized the map. I have a two-mile run to the first cluster of buildings that mark the entrance to town. After my sprint through Torrey Pines State Park, this should be a piece of cake. I shed my jacket and leave it on the front seat. I'm carrying my .38 and extra ammo on a leather Bianchi shoulder holster. I took a risk bringing it across the border, and it's no good against vampires, but Avery said there were humans here, too. I also have handcuffs and a Taser clipped to my belt. I don't know what effect the Taser might have on Donaldson, but I figure I can improvise when the time comes. And there's lots of wood littering the ground—stake material.

I'm as ready as I'll ever be.

The jog over the uneven ground is a little more difficult than I imagined, but only because I keep stumbling over rocks and the broken spines of fallen cacti. But in a few minutes, I see lights twinkling like fireflies in the distance. In another few minutes, I'm crouched behind the withered trunk of a scrub oak, peering down a dark ribbon of dirt that must be *Beso de la Muerte*'s main street. That light I spied earlier comes through the broken windows of a dilapidated saloon. Even from here, I can see holes in the corrugated tin roof, and the old fashioned swinging doors in front hang drunkenly on hinges twisted with time. The same shrill Corrido music that I listened to in the car pumps into the still air.

Obviously, Culebra's constituents aren't worried about keeping a low profile. There aren't any cars around, though, except for a shiny, black Expedition parked right in front. There's someone standing beside it, leaning against the driver's side door. He's tall, and the dark tank top he's wearing clings to a well-muscled torso as if painted on. He's smoking a cigar. The glowing tip rises and falls rhythmically as he raises it to his lips, then lowers it again to his side, flicking ash as he does. His face is obscured by shadow, and I watch him for a few minutes, trying to decide if I should make my way around to the back. I don't get a vampire vibe from him, and I need to get a look inside that saloon. If Donaldson is there, the plan is to wait for him to come out and follow him. If he isn't, I need to find my way to the tunnels.

Suddenly, the doors to the saloon swing outward and two men shoulder their way outside. The driver of the Expedition straightens and tosses the cigar into the street. He stands in respectful silence, watching as they approach the car.

The men are speaking Spanish and there's a lot of strutting and mutual back thumping, macho camaraderie suggesting a business deal well concluded. One of the men is dressed in a suit, the other, jeans and a poncho. It's not hard to imagine who belongs in the Expedition and who in the rundown saloon. Could Poncho be Culebra?

The suit turns to the driver and gestures with a hand. Immediately, the driver comes around to the passenger side and opens the rear door. When he does, the light from the car's interior shines on his face.

My heart thuds to a stop.

It's Max.

Max.

I can't believe it. Not that I don't believe Max's boss might be the gangster behind *Beso de la Muerte*. Wouldn't surprise me at all. What stuns me is the thought that if Max knows about this place, does he know about vampires as well?

I can do nothing but watch in a kind of bewildered stupor as the suit gets into the car, Max takes his position behind the wheel, and the car pulls away. Poncho stands with a hand frozen in farewell until the car disappears from sight. Then he drops his hand and spits noisily at the street. His gaze sweeps the distance until it seems to come to rest directly on me.

I know he can't see me. I'm crouched behind the tree and well into the shadows. And a probe of his mind tells me he's not vampire. Still, it's eerie to have those beady eyes seemingly fixed right on my position. He just stares for a minute or two, then spits again and pushes his way back inside the saloon.

If I still breathed, I'd be sighing with relief. As it is, I have to pull my thoughts back from the momentous question of whether Max knows all about vampires and concentrate again on finding David.

I send out a careful probe of the saloon. I don't feel the same tingle I felt when Donaldson was close to me at the fire. Yet, there are vampires inside. I detect four. Three are "speaking" Spanish and one some kind of Gallic dialect, French, maybe, yet, I understand their thoughts perfectly.

Imagine that. Vampire thought language.

Better than Esperanto.

And they're all thinking about the same thing—a lady inside with humongous tits.

But Donaldson isn't among the vampires inside.

Time for Plan B.

From Avery's map, I know I need to head behind the saloon to find the entrance to the tunnels. Since the saloon seems to be the only occupied building among the twenty or so sagging structures lining the street, it isn't difficult to slip undetected into the darkness beyond. It's amazing how clearly I can see. Every rock, cactus, and bush is outlined in a kind of eerie glow. I can even spot the black hole about half a mile away that must be the tunnel entrance. There are no lights, torch or electric, to mark it, and it hardly looks like the doorway to the bustling community Avery described.

Still, as I approach I detect a low hum. A generator, maybe? And I realize the "dark hole" I saw earlier is really a huge rock. It makes a perfect camouflaged doorway, covering the entrance completely except for a man-sized opening to the rear.

I'm almost inside when I hear footsteps coming toward me. I duck back out of sight and send out a cautious probe. It's a vampire, all right. The moment I sense that, I sense something else, too. It's Donaldson.

It seems that Avery's hunch was right.

He's alone, stepping out of the tunnel and heading with a determined stride toward the saloon. It's the first time I've been this close to him since the night he attacked me. I never thought to ask Avery how long Donaldson has been a vampire, but he looks different from his mug shot. He's lean rather than skinny and more confident in a predatory sort of way. His glasses are gone, too. Avery said to expect physical and mental changes to occur over and above the most obvious one—the need for blood. Perhaps this is what he meant—things such as sight, strength and speed are improved. In Donaldson's case, not a good thing.

Yet Donaldson's thoughts are strangely passive. I have to be careful how I probe, but I detect no anger or dark longings. There are no thoughts of David or of me. In fact, he seems only interested in getting to that lady with the big tits, too. Not to harm her. Well, at least not in the normal sense. He's experiencing a powerful lust that's almost embarrassing to tap in on.

Hardly the thoughts of a ruthless killer.

Still, if he's a psycho or sociopath, this is exactly how he would be acting. And I can't discount what he did to me.

I decide to let him go on to the saloon and search the tunnels. As long as our buxom friend is holding court there, I'll know where to find him.

CHAPTER 22

P AST THE ROCK, THE TUNNEL ENTRANCE YAWNS
open. There are lights here. Electric lamps hang on
hooks that stretch past my line of sight like a string of
over-sized Christmas lights. There are no hiding places,
though, so if I meet anyone I'll have two choices—talk
my way in, or subdue them with the Taser.

I unclip the Taser from my belt and hold it at the
ready.

I hug the wall, following it until it forks about a quarter of a mile in. The fork to the left is dark, the lights
continue to the right. I do, too. It's damp inside, and
smells of earth and the musk of compressed humanity,
but so far, I've seen no one. Nor have I heard the hum of
conversation, or picked up on a stray vampire commu-
nication. The place seems deserted.

Cautiously, I creep forward. I come upon compart-
ments hung with blankets that seem to be living quarters.

There are piles of personal belongings in each—clothes, shoes, the occasional book, radios, even a television or two, though I can't imagine what the reception would be like in the bowels of a mine. Beds consist of piles of straw; hot plates and canned goods provide sustenance. Except for the vampire lairs, of course. There are no hot plates in those. I wonder if the vamps go outside *Beso de la Muerte* to take their meals or if they've worked out some kind of deal to feed off their neighbors. For a price, I'm sure.

There's a makeshift medical ward, too, set up like a MASH unit with a couple of stainless steel gurneys and those racks that hold IV and blood lines. A cabinet along the back and a refrigerator are the only other things in the room. Not much in the way of medical technology—no monitors or computers. Of course, a criminal ending up here with a medical emergency couldn't expect much more.

I turn away and make another sweep, trying to determine which vamp bedroom is Donaldson's. I find it when I spy a picture of Donaldson with his wife and kiddies tucked atop a pile of magazines beside his bed. It seems very out of place, not only because it's in a cave, but also because I had the impression Donaldson had left that world behind. Why would he hold onto a picture that could only remind him of what he'd chosen to abandon?

I'll have to ask him when I get my hands on him.

I poke around, but there's nothing to indicate that David is here. I don't know what I expected to find, but something should point to his presence. Even if only food or water. The fact that there isn't anything at all brings back a familiar feeling of dread. Has Donaldson already killed him? Is David lying hurt somewhere in the desert outside the tunnel?

There's only one way to find out.

Now I have a decision to make. Should I wait for Donaldson to return from the saloon or should I go get him? I'm debating this as I work my way back to the tunnel entrance. I've still seen no one, and it's downright spooky. Is everyone in the saloon? Have some left to go to town? Avery never said how many desperados made *Beso de la Muerte* their home, but from the looks of their "living" quarters, I expected more than the fifteen or twenty I estimate to be here. Doesn't seem to be any women, either. I guess female desperados don't find the idea of living like a bat in a damp cave very appealing.

Except for Miss Mammaries back there in the saloon, of course.

Which brings me back to Donaldson. I could summon him with a vamp signal. But would he alone catch it, or would the other vampires pick up on it, too? I don't want to be distracted or attacked by a mob. I just want Donaldson.

So I hunker down behind the saloon and wait. The desert air has turned cool, but the sand beneath my feet retains the warmth of the day. I send out tentative probes to see how he's doing with the girl in the bar. All I get in response is that same, lascivious carnal longing now fueled to greater heights by alcohol. He's hanging out with the other vampires and they're placing bets about who will bed her tonight. If she has a choice in the matter, it doesn't come up.

After an hour, my patience is at an end. Donaldson shows no sign of making his move so I make mine. I let myself into Donaldson's head, at first just a gentle prod to let him know someone is reaching out to him.

He responds immediately. *I knew there was someone there. Who are you?*

I wish I could see his face, read his reaction. But I can't, so there's no choice but to continue.

Come outside and see.

A snort. *I don't think so. You come inside.*

I don't like crowds. Our business is private.

What business?

You'll find out when we meet.

What's in it for me?

What do you want?

There's a pause while he considers his answer. I use the time to regroup. It's hard work to keep all traces of my identity out of our conversation. When he sees me for the first time, I want it to be a surprise. How he reacts will tell me a lot.

What do you look like?

What?

What do you look like? I want to know if what you have to offer is worth giving up what I have going in here.

Jesus. Typical male. Thinks with his dick. Maybe I can use it to my advantage.

I put a purr in my voice. *You didn't have any complaints the last time we were together.*

In spite of the alcohol, I sense his interest level spike. *So, we've met before?*

That's one way of putting it. *Yes.*

There's a grin in his voice. *Where did you say you were?*

Right outside. In back.

I'll be right there.

He closes his mind, which puts me at a disadvantage. I'm assuming he's doing it so his friends won't pick up on his plans, but since it shuts me out, too, I don't like it.

I take out the Taser again and hold it at the ready. There doesn't seem to be a back door, which means Donaldson will be coming either from the right or the left around the building. There's no cover, either, and Donaldson's night vision will allow him to see me at the same moment I see him. Maybe I should have arranged the meeting back at the tunnel.

Too late to change plans now.

The saloon doors creak open. I crouch down, waiting for the sound of footsteps to tell me which direction he's coming from.

One minute passes, then two.

There are no footsteps.

What's he doing? Has he changed his mind? Is he standing on the steps smoking a frigging cigar while he decides whether or not to meet me? Should I ask him?

No need, Anna. I'm right here.

The voice is so close, it reverberates in my head like a scream. I've been so concentrated on the front, his appearance from behind comes completely without warning.

Just like before.

But this time, I don't drop the Taser and I don't let his sudden presence put me off guard. I straighten and turn to face him.

So you recognize me.

He smiles, a complacent, tight-lipped little smile. *Oh, yes.*

Then you know why I'm here.

Is it because you enjoyed my technique so much the first time that you've come back for an encore? Oh wait, no need. You took what you wanted from me. You know, I'm the one who should feel violated. I just wanted a simple roll in the hay. Look what you turned it into.

I'm shaking with fury. The urge to kill him is so strong that it's only the image of David in my head keeping me from attacking him.

Forcefully, I calm myself, motioning at him with the Taser. *Let's take a walk.*

But he doesn't seem the least bit concerned by the Taser or by my thoughts. *Why would I want to take a walk with you?*

Because if you don't, I'm going to blast you with this thing and drag you into the bushes where I'll happily bash your head in with a rock.

He clucks his tongue. *My, my. That's an awful lot of attitude for a little girl.*

He's baiting me and I'm swallowing it. I have to drag myself back from the anger threatening my good sense. Being this close to the bastard who threw my life into such disarray is having a much more profound effect on me than I expected. I have to remind myself why I'm here. David.

He picks through all this and finally reacts. *Who's David?*

That triggers another spasm of blind rage. *Don't play with me, Donaldson. Believe me, I'd love nothing better than to kill you. The only reason I haven't already is because you're going to tell me what you've done with David.*

He reflects a moment, searching my thoughts. *David? Oh, the guy from the bar. Now that was a dirty trick. And I saw you with him at the fire, didn't I?*

Which is another thing I have to thank you for, you miserable bastard. Why'd you do it? You must have known I wasn't inside. Even if you hadn't gone in, you would have felt it.

He's shaking his head at me, as if I'm speaking gibberish. *I don't know where you're getting your information, but you need a new source. I didn't set that fire. I didn't even know it was your home.*

Oh. Right. You just happened to be in the neighborhood when it burned.

As a matter of fact, yes. I was summoned. I don't know by whom. But when I saw you, I beat it out of there. I figured you would be a little pissed at me for—well, you know.

Donaldson, you're a damned liar, but you're right about seriously pissing me off. I don't give a shit about the fire right now. I want to know where you've taken David.

I told you, I don't know anything about your friend.

That does it. I step right up to him, pushing the Taser at his gut. *If I pull this trigger, I wonder what*

*will happen? Will you jump and wiggle like a fish on a
hook or just drop like a rock? Either way works for me.*

He still isn't reacting with anything close to fear. In
fact, blind indifference is the only emotion bubbling to
the surface. It only makes me angrier. I have the Taser
on contact stun and I pull the trigger.

A Taser shoots 50,000 volts of energy at .162 amps to
penetrate the nervous system and render the victim im-
mobile. It doesn't matter where you aim either, because
the entire body is covered with a neural net. I have the
thing shoved right into Donaldson's midsection when I
fire, yet I'm not getting the reaction I expect.

In fact, I'm getting no reaction at all.

He's staring down at me with a puzzled expression
that turns almost immediately into a derisive grin. *Oh,
Anna, Anna. You have so much to learn.*

Then he backhands me with a wallop that sends me
flying into the dirt. It's so unexpected that it takes me a
minute to shake away the cobwebs. But he doesn't follow up, which I'm going to make him regret. I jump to
my feet, blood pounding with rage. I feel it in my head
and coursing through my body, an unrestrained fury. It's
feral and ugly and it's going to allow me to do what I
should have done the moment Donaldson appeared.

When I attack this time, it's with my fists and teeth.
He's taken by surprise at the ferocity, but he recovers
quickly. He's holding back, making the mistake of thinking he's stronger because he's male. He's forgetting an
important fact of nature. The female is always the best
hunter, often the more brutal. When I come at him, he
tries to parry the blows, to step out of my reach. I don't

let him. I keep inside, putting every ounce of vampire strength into each punch. I aim at his stomach with my hands, his throat with my teeth. I can wear him down—he has the disadvantage of having consumed a lot of beer—but I don't want to take the time. With a final, decisive thrust, I have him down on his back in the dirt. I'm pummeling his stomach, my teeth at his jugular.

Hey, Donaldson, are you awake? I want you awake. It's no fun otherwise.

For the first time, I detect a little concern percolating through the drunken haze in Donaldson's head. It's finally dawning on him that he doesn't have the upper hand. He starts to send out an "SOS" to his pals in the saloon, but I stop that with a snarl. My teeth are at his neck.

Don't. I'll tear your throat out. It's a little trick I learned from you.

He backs off, his mind closing down. *What do you want?*

I told you. I want to know where you've taken David.

And I told you, I don't have him. Look, check it out. You can get into my head. What do you see?

I use no finesse this time. I hold his head against the dirt and stab into his thoughts with the power of a blow torch. I read confusion at what's happening; aggravation that I've overpowered him; smugness that he could take me if he really wanted to; lust at the feeling of my pelvis pressing against his crotch. He starts squirming under me as that last thought provokes a physical reaction.

God. Donaldson, you're a pervert.

He starts to sit up, but I push him back down. This

time, I have my arm across his throat. I'm still not convinced he doesn't have David. And it's lowering my tolerance level more each minute.

He senses that I've reached the end of my patience. He tries to shake me off, but I'm not about to let him go. I press my elbow against his jugular. It's instinctive, I guess. If he was a mortal, I'd go for the windpipe, but since we vampires don't breathe, it makes sense that pressure on the jugular would produce the same result.

It does. When I feel him on the verge of losing consciousness, I ease off just enough to let my voice ring through.

Where is he?

Donaldson chokes and shakes his head.

I apply pressure again.

Where is he?

This time, there's real panic in his voice. *I don't know. You have to believe me. I didn't take him. Why would I?*

To get me here, asshole. To finish what you started in that parking lot.

What sense does that make? You're no threat to me. Just the opposite. You're on top.

It rings true. Yet I don't want to believe him. If he doesn't have David, who does?

I think I know.

What?

I think I know who may have your friend.

I lean back a little to see his face. *If this is just bullshit, Donaldson—*

No. Get off me and I'll tell you.

I don't think so. I think you'll tell me now.

My elbow is back at his throat. I lean into it. His head swims. I detect little pinpoints of exploding light. It's just like watching fireworks. Interesting. I press a little harder.

Donaldson's eyes are wide; the alarm reflected in his head "tastes" like a potent cocktail, part adrenaline, part fear. I savor it; let it roll over my own thoughts, become part of my own consciousness. It's a great feeling. Powerful. Sexy. I understand the connection between power and sex now. The realization that I can snuff out a life— even one as worthless as Donaldson's—is heady stuff.

Anna, enough.

The same voice that came to me at Avery's is back. My own voice. I respond the same way.

I don't want to stop.

You have to. You can't kill him.

Why not?

Because it's wrong.

Not good enough.

Then think about what happens to David if you kill him. He says he may know who has him.

He's probably lying.

Can you take that chance?

Reluctantly, I ease up. *No.*

I roll off him and lie staring into a cold, dark sky. I feel him beside me, gathering strength. When I'm sure he's recovered enough to answer my question, I yank him into a sitting position.

This is your last chance. Who has David?

But before he can answer, there is a whine, like the

whir of an insect. Donaldson jerks under my hands. He looks down at his chest in disbelief.

I follow his gaze. The point of an arrow protrudes through his shirt. His mouth opens and closes, like a fish struggling to breathe air. I look on in disbelief as he crumbles under my grip, falling in on himself, dissolving finally in a cloud of ash that gusts away as a breath of air blows over us.

It happens just that quickly, and then he's gone.

CHAPTER 23

IT TAKES A SECOND TO GRASP WHAT HAPPENED. But in that second I become aware of a stirring somewhere in front of me, deep in the shadows. I hear the click of a crossbow as it is cocked and know I have only an instant to respond before that humming translates into an arrow honing in on my chest.

I dive for a small clump of rocks, the only cover available. I hunker down, trying to make myself small. The humming comes closer and an arrow whizzes over my head.

Fear clutches at my throat. I send out a probe to see if I can pick up on anything, identify the attacker. But nothing comes back. I can't even tell if my attacker is human or vamp, male or female.

Not that it makes any difference. A wooden arrow through the heart is fatal no matter who's holding the crossbow.

The bow is cocked again. Acute hearing isn't always a blessing. I brace myself, burrowing into the dirt like a mole. Again the buzzing and the silent breath of air as the arrow whistles past. How long is he going to keep trying?

The question is answered a heartbeat later when another arrow flies toward me. This time, though, the aim has improved. I cry out as the arrow buries itself in the calf of my left leg. I've been concentrating on protecting my upper body. My hiding place left my legs exposed. Obviously, something that didn't go unnoticed.

Red-hot pain radiates upward until it centers somewhere in my chest. It's not a fatal shot, but it's definitely going to slow me down when and if I can make a break for it.

I reach down and yank. I have first-hand experience about how quickly we vampires heal but it still hurts like a son of a bitch when that arrow tears through. Tears of pain and anger burn my cheeks. I hold on to the arrow, thinking it will make a good weapon if whoever's out there is a vampire and comes closer for the kill shot.

I hope he does. Besides the arrow, I slip my gun out of the holster. I'm ready for anything now.

But nothing happens. No more arrows. No sound of footsteps. The only thing I hear is the music from the cantina behind me, obliterated from my consciousness until now by the intensity of my concentration on the attacker. I'm pretty sure he's gone. My vamp warning system has gone inert, no more DEFCON sirens blaring in my head.

With a groan of relief, I lie back on the sand, massaging torn calf muscles. There's the warm, viscous feel of blood on my fingers. Curious, I raise the hand to my lips and taste.

Then the complete grossness of what I did hits. I can't believe I just tasted my own blood.

Still.

The fingers dip for another sample.

It's not too bad.

Anna, get a grip.

My little voice is back. And with it, a wave of sorrow that shakes my very core.

David.

I'm no closer to finding him. Donaldson was my only hope. The only thing I've learned from this fiasco is that I'm pretty certain he was telling me the truth. He didn't kidnap David.

But he thought he knew who did.

Or so he said.

Jesus.

Cautiously, I pull myself into a sitting position. When I scan the area, I pick up nothing but desert. Nothing living except things that scamper, skitter, or slither. It makes even my dead skin crawl.

I consider corralling one of Donaldson's vamp pals to corroborate his story. In this place, having a kidnap victim would be currency, like money in the bank. Maybe he bragged about it, even let on where he was holding the guy.

But I doubt it. Donaldson was completely vulnerable

to my little mind fuck and he gave nothing away. And he was really scared at the end. He knew I wanted to kill him.

There's nothing more for me to do here. With another groan, I pick myself up. My right leg gives a little when I try to put weight on it, but it holds. I know I won't be jogging back to the car, but I can walk.

Still clutching the arrow in one hand and the gun in the other, I limp out of *Beso de la Muerte*.

It takes me a lot longer to get back to the car than it did to reach Donaldson's hideout. Even with vampire healing, the pain limits me to a sedate hobble. I snatch up a dead branch to use as a crutch, but it's not much help. All I get for my effort is a hand full of splinters.

Forty-five long minutes later, I reach the Explorer. Thankfully, it's still where I left it. I don't think I could have walked all the way to Tijuana. This time, I shrug off the holster and lock up my gun and the handcuffs in the glove compartment. I don't know how I'll explain my bloody leg if I'm stopped at the border, but I don't want to complicate matters by getting caught with a gun. I don't have a clue what happened to the Taser. I suppose it's lying somewhere in the dirt in back of the saloon. It wasn't much help anyway.

Now all I want to do is go home.

Go home.

And where exactly is home?

A pall settles over me as I get back on the road. I still have no clue where David is or how he is. I'd figured Donaldson was the only one who had motive to take him. Now I'm back to square one. Worse than square one. Who else hates me enough to do this? David and I brought in a lot of fugitives in the last couple of years, but we're relatively new in the business. All of our collars who were convicted are still cooling their heels in prisons around the country. Of course, it could be the relatives of someone we turned in. But what would be the point of that? Especially since no one came forward to take credit. Doesn't make sense.

The border crossing approaches and I glance down to see how bad my leg looks. I'm glad it's my left leg, the one closest to the door, because it's dark and in the shadows, where it's not possible to detect the torn pants or dark smears of blood. It's very late, too, almost three in the morning, and the bored guard asks the perfunctory questions of place of birth and if I have anything to declare.

I force a smile and say, "San Diego, California, and no, nothing to declare."

When he waves me through, I'm tempted to add, "Except for the fact that I've just spent the night looking for my kidnapped friend in one of Mexico's lesser known tourist spots, where I was shot with an arrow and almost dusted. On top of all that, I'm no closer to finding my friend because the vampire who I thought kidnapped him said he didn't know anything about it, and now he's dead so I'll never know for sure. I'm so tired, I can hardly keep my eyes open. It'll be a miracle if I even make it back to Avery's. And, oh yeah, there's one more thing. I hope to God I never have to come back here. Ever."

But, of course, getting hysterical in front of a Mexican border guard wouldn't be in my best interest, so those declarations I keep to myself.

CHAPTER 24

I HEAD FOR AVERY'S. I DON'T KNOW WHERE ELSE to go. I have no home. I can't bear the thought of being at David's without him. Avery was right about where to find Donaldson. Maybe he can help me figure out what to do next.

Later this morning I will go back to David's to see if I've missed something—anything to indicate what might have happened to him. I'll bring in the police, too. I can't let any more time go by without asking for help.

My leg throbs. The pain is a good traveling companion, though. It keeps me awake. I realize it's been two full days since I've gotten any real sleep. The night I spent with Avery, we didn't get much rest.

Which brings my thoughts to Max. Seeing him in *Beso de la Muerte* fills me with questions. Could he know about the existence of vampires? Or is he only aware that his boss uses the place as a hideout for his henchmen? It would open up a world of possibilities if Max were accepting of vampires.

But my saner voice knows it is unlikely he will be. Especially if the only vampires he has contact with are the ones in that godforsaken place.

And besides, when he learns what I've done with Avery—

I don't want to even think about it.

Instead, I go on autopilot, concentrating on the drive up Soledad Mountain Road. I've made this trip so many times in the last forty-eight hours, I don't have to think about it. I seem to be making this a habit, appearing at his doorstep in the middle of the night. I hope Avery is awake and doesn't mind my crashing at his home tonight. In that big house, he's bound to have a guestroom.

But I don't even get as far as the front door. Avery appears at the car the minute I pull up. He must have been waiting for me because he's dressed in jeans and a sweatshirt, the sleeves rolled past his elbows. His face is full of anxious concern when he sees my leg.

"What happened?" he asks, sweeping me into his arms as if I were a doll.

"Wow," I say, so surprised by being picked up that way I actually let him carry me. "You *must* have been worried. This is quite a reaction. You're actually *speaking* to me—with your voice."

He brings me into the living room and settles me on a couch facing the fireplace.

"How did you know I'd be back tonight?"

He's kneeling at my side, worrying at the cuffs of my jeans until he rips the seam open to expose the wound. He answers without looking up. "You mean because I'm dressed? I didn't. I just got back from the hospital." His full attention is on the wound, turning my leg this way and that until he seems satisfied about something. Then he sits back on his heels and faces me. "The arrow went clean through."

I feel the hair stir on the back of my neck. I raise myself onto my elbows. "How did you know it was an arrow?"

He gives me another of those slow-student looks. "I've been a doctor for two hundred years. I know what an arrow wound looks like. You shouldn't have pulled it out, you know. It would have been a lot less painful if you'd left it for me to remove."

"Oh." I sink back into the cushions. "Right. And how do I explain an arrow sticking out of my leg to the border guards? Ran into a little trouble with the natives?"

He ignores my remark and bends his head to my leg. He places his mouth over the torn skin and sucks gently.

"Wow. This is kinky."

He ignores that, too, his tongue tracing the edges of the injury until I feel a tingle that starts deep in my calf muscle and radiates outward. He continues to probe the wound, and the sensation is so pleasurable that I stop fighting it and let my head drop back onto the cushion. He starts singing me a little lullaby in his head—a *lullaby* of all things—and before I can comment on it, I'm fast asleep.

THE NEXT THING I KNOW, I'M BEING AWAKENED BY a gentle touch on my arm. I drag myself from sleep reluctantly, thinking for a minute that I'm in my own home, in my own bed, and that it's Max nudging me awake.

"No, Anna. It's not Max." Avery is speaking in a soft voice, smoothing my hair back off my forehead. "Sorry."

I open my eyes and give Avery a rueful smile and struggle into a sitting position. I'm still on the couch, an afghan so soft it must be made of cashmere thrown over me. "You have nothing to be sorry for. Thanks for taking me in last night."

He holds out a cup of coffee. When I take it, he asks, *How does your leg feel?*

I take a sip of the coffee and hand him back the cup so that I can push the afghan out of the way. When I look down at my calf, I can hardly believe my eyes. There's not even a bruise to mark where the arrow penetrated.

"Too bad you can't do this with mortal patients. It's quite a trick."

He laughs. *Well, you had something to do with it, too. You are remarkably strong.*

He pauses a moment, letting me readjust myself on the couch before he asks. *What happened? I can only assume you didn't find David.*

No. I let him pick the memory out of my head, sadness descending again, coloring my thoughts with a despair I don't try to disguise.

Avery reads my feelings, tries to offer what comfort he can. *With Donaldson dead, what will you do now?*

Go back to David's. Look around some more. See if I've missed anything. If not— I shrug. "I guess I'll have to call the police."

He nods. *I'll give you Chief Williams' private number. I've told him what we know, but so far he's learned nothing from his contacts. David seems to have disappeared off the face of the Earth.*

It's not exactly what I want to hear. I push off the couch. *I think I left my bag here yesterday, didn't I?*

Avery motions toward the stairs. *I took the liberty of putting your things in a bedroom upstairs. I hope you don't mind.*

I stand on tiptoe and give him a kiss on the cheek. *You've been a good friend.*

A good friend? He puts his hands on my shoulders and kisses me back, hard, on the lips. *Is that all?*

But this isn't the time and my thoughts are too conflicted to give him a proper answer. He reads the signals, lets his hands drop and takes a step back. He does smile, though, and points again to the stairs.

First door to the left—across from my bedroom. By the time you've showered, I'll have breakfast waiting.

I trudge up the stairs wondering how I'll ever repay him for all the help he's given me.

His voice follows me. *We'll think of something.*

The guestroom is large, the walls painted a pale

yellow. Delicate lace curtains move in the breeze of an open window. Bright morning sun is reflected in the gleam of polished mahogany and off the glass in frames of wonderful old oil paintings that look vaguely familiar. Old masters, I'm betting, and originals, not copies. Avery even unpacked my bag. I find my clothes folded neatly in an armoire. I had no toiletries with me, but the adjoining bathroom is well stocked. With feminine toiletries. Perfumed shampoos and bath oils.

Did he do this for me or does the good doctor have lots of female visitors?

Not really my business, is it? I should be grateful for what's here.

And I am. A shower and clean clothes revive my body if not my spirit. Avery has eggs and bacon and toast waiting for me when I come back down. The smell triggers a visceral response—my stomach actually growls I'm so hungry.

Avery has set places at a small table in the corner of a big kitchen. It's like a restaurant kitchen with stainless steel appliances and acres of spotless white tile. He holds my chair for me and I sink into it.

I pick up my fork and look over at his place. There's nothing except a cup full of dark liquid. *You're not eating?*

He holds up the cup. *This is all I need.*

I start in on the eggs, but after only two bites, I push the plate away. *I guess I'm not hungry after all.*

Avery looks at me for a long moment, then stands up and goes to the refrigerator. He takes a pitcher out, pours a cup from it and places the cup in the microwave.

After thirty seconds, the timer chimes and he brings the cup over to me.

The liquid in the cup is a dark, thick, unmistakable red. I raise an eyebrow. *I assume this isn't V8?*

He laughs. *No. It's blood.*

The eyebrow ratchets higher. *Blood? Human Blood?*

No, pig's blood. Of course, it's human blood.

I find myself looking around the kitchen suspiciously. *Avery, where did you get human blood?*

From the servants I keep chained in the basement. Everyday, I drain just enough from them to sustain my own life and prolong theirs.

At first fear, a cold, creepy thrust of it, knocks me off balance. Then I see the twinkle in his eye and feel the laughter bubbling just beneath the surface of his mind.

It's a good thing I don't have my gun. I'd be tempted to shoot you for that.

He lets the laughter erupt. *For a tough cookie, you are so easy.*

I finger the cup, sniff the contents. *This smells like blood.*

I told you it is. But don't worry. I get it from the hospital blood bank. When we have blood that is going to expire before we can use it, a tech friend of mine gives it to me. It would be thrown out anyway, so why not put it to good use?

But I thought it's not the kind of blood we need.

Technically, no. You couldn't subsist on it for any length of time. But you fed from me just a day or so ago, so you don't need real nourishment. It looks to me as if your taste for regular food is just about gone, too, but you obviously needed something. Think of this as a pick-me-up.

He pauses, a delicate question forming in his head.

No, I answer. *I didn't feed from Donaldson. Not that I wouldn't have torn out his throat if he hadn't cooperated. Somebody killed him before I had the chance.*

We drink then in desultory silence. The blood has a strange taste. When I drank from Avery, his blood was suffused with life, rich and robust. This is—

"Musty tasting," Avery explains, reading my reaction. "Like the difference between a fine old wine and a cheap upstart. When you drink from a living creature, you take more than sustenance. You take their life essence. Refrigerated blood loses that spark very quickly. It's why we can't exist on it indefinitely. But it is blood and in an emergency, it has its uses."

"This is an emergency?"

Avery puts his cup down and reaches across the table to take my hand. "You've had a rough night. And I'm afraid what you face today won't be much easier."

I fear that, too. My thoughts are weighed down by the knowledge that I'm no closer to finding David than I was before I went to *Beso de la Muerte.*

Avery squeezes my hand. "What would you do if David was a fugitive?"

I'm caught off guard by his question. "What?"

"What would you do if you were looking for him because he was wanted by the law?"

I put down my cup and purse my lips. *Well, I'd run a credit card check, see if he's bought a plane ticket or made hotel reservations somewhere. I'd call his friends—*

My eyes seek Avery's. Gloria. *She's in New York.*

Avery nods, but just as quickly, I shake my head.

He's not with Gloria. He wouldn't have left knowing I was on my way. I'm the reason he stayed in San Diego in the first place.

What else would you do?

Impatiently, I push away from the table and stand up. *It's not the same. There was blood in his condo. His wallet and keys were there. The front door was open. David didn't leave willingly. He was taken. The question is why?*

I've gathered up my breakfast things and taken them to the sink. Avery waves me off.

Leave the dishes. My housekeeper will be here in a little while.

But I need something to do, even if it's only a mundane thing like rinsing dishes. When I've stowed everything in the dishwasher, I turn back to Avery.

Do you think Chief Williams will help me if I call him?

Of course. Avery pulls a small notebook out of his pocket along with a silver ballpoint pen. He flips to a blank page and starts writing. Then he tears the page off and hands it to me.

"I've already called him and explained the situation. I've included my office number here, too. If you need me today, call. I'll be at the hospital until six, but I'll leave word that you should be put straight through."

I fold the paper into my jeans pocket. "I've another favor to ask. Do you suppose I could borrow the Explorer again? If someone is waiting for me at David's, they might be looking for my car."

He points to a spot on the counter. "Help yourself. The keys are right there."

I gather them up and turn to go.

Thank you, Avery. Again.

Anytime, Anna.

He comes around the table and wraps me in a hug. *You know I want to help. I just wish there was more I could do.*

I let my head rest a moment against his chest, drawing strength. Then I straighten up. *Wish me luck.*

He smiles. *You've got it.*

CHAPTER 25

W HEN I GET TO THE CONDO, I RING THE BELL,
hoping irrationally that David will be there to
answer the door. I won't even mind the tongue-lashing
he's sure to give me for not showing up last night.

But I know deep down he won't be there and, of
course, he isn't.

After a moment, I use his own keys to let myself in,
amazed that I thought to grab them before leaving yesterday considering the shape I was in.

Everything is exactly as I remember it.

I make a sweep of the entire condo, a thorough sweep
this time, before coming back to the dining room. The
blood on the corner of the table has dried to black flakes.
Thankfully, there isn't a lot of it. Of course, if David was
captured by a vampire, there wouldn't be. I push that
thought out of my head.

After I've stared at the blood for ten minutes and no useful idea how I might proceed presents itself, I dial Chief Williams. He answers himself, surprising me into speechlessness for a moment until I remember that Avery said this was a private line.

"Chief Williams, this is Anna Strong."

A deep-timbered voice comes back across the line. "Dr. Avery said you might call. Nothing from your friend?"

"No. And I'm really worried. Do you suppose you could send someone to meet me at his condo? I need a professional cop's opinion. I'm out of my depth here."

"I can be there in ten minutes. What's the address?"

I give him the address and unit number and tell him I'll buzz him in. He hangs up and I stare at the phone for a moment. He's coming himself? Not a good sign, I'm sure.

When Williams arrives, he's alone and in civilian clothes. Another surprise. He shakes my hand and explains, "This is my day off."

He follows me inside, and his gray-green eyes scan the interior. It's lightning fast but I get the impression he's not missing much. His mind is closed, allowing me the freedom to size him up at close range, something I didn't do at the party. He's tall, over six feet, but not as tall as David. He's much leaner, too, a vampire trait, I've discovered. Must be the liquid protein diet. He's wearing jeans and a polo shirt topped by a leather bomber jacket, worn Nike sports shoes on his feet. His hair is dark, but flecked with gray. I wonder if that's an affectation. I don't know how old he is, but I would imagine a police chief would be at least in his fifties. Williams' face is unlined for the most part. Can't do anything about that if you're a vampire, but at least your hair can "age."

He turns those sharp eyes on me. He lifts a hand and runs it through his hair. *Does it look natural? It's a bitch trying to convince a hair stylist that you want gray in your hair when the majority of their clientele is devoted to taking it out.*

Very natural. I wave a hand. *What do you think?*

Williams walks out on the balcony before responding. *Nice view.*

Nice view? I follow him onto the deck. *Chief Williams, my friend is missing. I'm very concerned about him. I need your opinion about what to do. Should I file a missing person's report? Should I start contacting his friends and family? I'm at my wit's end here. I really need your help.*

Williams takes a cigar case from the inside pocket of his jacket, takes his time extracting a fat cigar, and rolls it between his fingers before finally bringing it to his lips. He bites off the tip and spits it over the balcony. Then he breaks out a lighter and puffs away until the tip glows.

During all this, I'm shifting from one foot to the other, swallowing back my impatience and fighting down a wave of anger. When he's finally completed the cigar ritual, he raises indifferent eyes to mine.

David is a mortal.

He sounds suspiciously like Avery. *And what's your point?*

We don't get involved in mortal affairs. Not when it involves the possibility that our identities could be revealed in the course of an investigation.

Our identities? Just whose identity are you worried about?

He makes himself comfortable on a deck chair and leans back, the hand with the cigar resting on the arm. He acts like this is a social visit.

I know how serious this is to you. I just don't know what I can do to help.

Well, let me tell you. You can act like a cop. You can help me file a report, put out an APB on David, act like you give a damn that my best friend and partner is missing. Those things would be a good start.

Williams' eyes turn hard. *My getting involved would be a mistake.*

Why?

Because it's very possible your friend was taken in retaliation for your escaping the Revengers the other night. If that's the case, opening an investigation won't help. It will only call attention to the fact that you have influence in the police department. Not a good thing.

I stare at him a moment. *But it was a cop who stopped me. One of yours.*

Not one of mine, I assure you.

Williams climbs to his feet, flicks ash over the balcony railing, and turns to me. *Not a city cop. The Revengers are state patrolmen.*

He's right—a distinction I hadn't made until now.

Believe me, William's continues, *I do my best to discover their identities and weed them out.*

Weed them out? There's no mistaking what he's saying. *How do you manage that?*

He shrugs. *Accident, hot call goes bad. Fortunately, we haven't had to deal with it much lately. Donaldson's activity is what triggered this new rash of vampire hunting. It would have helped if you'd gotten a badge or car number.*

Well, forgive me for not thinking too clearly. I'd only been a vampire for a day or two and I wasn't expecting to be kidnapped. And if what you say is true, and the Revenger's took David, why haven't they contacted me? What would they want?

Their intention may simply be to persuade you to move on. It's not often they stumble on a vampire with close friends or family members to use as leverage. Most vampires are too old to have living relatives. In your case, though, there's David, your parents. I think Avery mentioned a boyfriend, too.

At that, what little patience I have left melts like ice cream under the heat of mounting hostility toward Chief Williams. "Are you saying they'll go after my parents next? Or my boyfriend? And there's nothing you can do about it?"

Williams holds up a hand. "What I'm saying is that there may not be anything I can do about it. You got the better of them, not something that happens very often. But look what's happened since. You've lost your home. Your partner is missing. It's very possible that if you leave San Diego, relocate somewhere else, David might be released."

"*Might* be released. You don't know that for sure."

No. I don't know anything for sure, including if they even have David. But what alternative do you have? I know this isn't easy, but sometimes the best thing a vampire can do is move on. We've all had to do it. Word will get around that Donaldson is gone and things will quiet down. It's even possible that you might be able to return to San Diego in a year or two.

And what do I tell my parents in the meantime?

Tell them the truth. Your home has been destroyed. What do you really have to tie you here? I understand from Dr. Avery that relations between you and your family are strained.

How does he know that? Then I remember. Avery was probably reading my thoughts at the hospital from the moment I came in. But that doesn't explain why he would share them with Williams.

Williams shrugs. *He thought I should know. It might help me to persuade you to do the right thing.*

And that's to leave San Diego.

For the time being. Let things cool down.

And this is really what Avery wants?

At that, Williams turns away from me, shielding his eyes and his thoughts from my scrutiny. Finally, he says softly, "Avery has developed a soft spot for you. He isn't thinking too clearly right now. He needs a cooler head to prevail, which is why he had you contact me. He knew I could be impersonal about this situation where he cannot."

"So, he doesn't want me to leave?"

Williams doesn't answer.

It rankles, but I don't see that I have any option except to go along with him, at least for now. "Do you have any way to get a message to the Revengers?"

Williams looks at me, eyebrow raised. "Why?"

"Because I'm willing to do as you request, but only after David is released unharmed."

His eyes narrow. "Do you mean that?"

"Does that mean you can get a message to them?"

"If I answer that, in a court of law, it would be an admission that I know who they are. I'm not saying that I do."

Spoken like a damned lawyer. I snap, "How badly do you want me gone?"

Williams shifts away from the balcony, crossing into the living room. At the door, he pauses. He doesn't look around, but his voice floats back across the quiet room. "I'll see what I can do. I'll call you at Avery's tonight."

I wait until the door is closed behind him to let my mind open. I don't trust him. He's evasive about the Revengers and too eager to get rid of me. My instincts tell me that as crazy as it sounds, he not only knows about the Revengers, he may very well be one of them. Which makes me wonder why Avery trusts him.

If he does.

But Avery is the one who suggested I contact Chief Williams.

My stomach churns with impatience. It doesn't make sense. Why would Avery do that? He doesn't act like he wants me gone, either, which is what Williams implied. And if the Revengers have David, why not just contact me and offer to make the switch—my life for David's?

What in hell is going on?

CHAPTER 26

I HAVE NO INTENTION OF SITTING IDLY BY, whiling away the hours until Williams gets back to me. But what to do? My first impulse is to call Avery, tell him everything that happened and see how he reacts.

But he is a doctor and there are patients who depend on him.

Reluctantly, I decide to drive out to Mission Beach and see what progress has been made on the arson investigation. I say reluctantly because I'm not sure I'm up to facing the devastation again. But it beats sitting alone at the condo or at Avery's wallowing in my fear. It's not much, but it gets me moving.

There's yellow police tape all around the property and a notice posted against the gate advising that this is a crime scene and to keep out. And yet, there are two teenage boys poking around the debris. I literally have to take a deep breath, no easy trick for a vampire, to calm myself before I approach them.

"Mind telling me what you guys are doing?"

The taller of the two turns to face me. He has a silver frame in his hands, what's left of a picture of my grandmother. "What's it to you?" he demands, puffing his chest like a preening pigeon.

I snatch the frame out of his hand and quick as lightning, back him into the fence. His face flashes a warning, but I'm quicker. I grab the fist he's aimed at my head and force it back to his side, squeezing his fingers together until he yelps in pain.

I wave the picture at him. "This is my property. I want you and your little friend off of it."

His "friend" joins us now, as full of himself as his partner was before I put the hurt on him. With no conscious effort on my part, I drop the frame, reach back, and jerk him into the fence, too. I've got both of them, squirming like toads and hurling invectives at me with a fervor I haven't heard since I taught high school. It makes me smile.

"Is there a problem here, ma'am?"

A cop on a bike with the face of an angel.

Who says there's never a cop around when you want one? I shove both boys out the gate. "Found these guys disturbing the crime scene. Since it used to be my home, I took umbrage."

The cop says a few words into the radio at his collar. Then he slips cuffs from his belt and locks the two kids around the fence post. "I'll take it from here. I've just called for a car. Are you all right?"

I've knelt down to retrieve the picture frame. There's nothing left of the photograph except scorched paper and melted glass. I'm as close to tears as I was in Avery's car right after the fire.

The cop seems to sense my distress. He puts a gentle hand on my elbow and helps me to my feet. "I'll make sure we keep a closer eye on your property, but you might want to hire a private security company. At least then you know there will be someone here twenty-four/seven."

I thank him and assure him I'll do just that.

Then the patrol car arrives and the two kids are bundled off. The bike cop resumes his patrol, leaving me alone to hug the frame and stare out at the ocean through tear-blurred eyes.

Sometimes the sorrow is overwhelming. It takes effort to fight it back. But David is still out there and I doubt I'm going to get much help from Williams, even if he calls me tonight and tells me it's all set. I won't believe David is safe until I see it for myself.

Which means I need an alternate plan of my own. I settle myself on the sea wall at the end of my block and force myself to think.

I make a mental list of the things I know for sure and the things I need to find out.

Number one—I know I'm a vampire because of Donaldson. So far, not such a good thing for me.

Number two—I'm pretty sure Donaldson had nothing to do with either the fire or David's kidnapping. I can't be positive of that, of course. I can never be positive because Donaldson is dead. I just have to conclude that he was too scared to lie back at *Beso de la Muerte*.

Number three—Why is Donaldson dead? Another Revenger attack? Did they follow me or was Donaldson the target all along? How can I find out?

Number four—I neither like nor trust Williams. He could easily have put that cop on my tail the other night after Avery's party. If he did, he wants me out of the way pretty badly. Our conversation this afternoon confirms that. He didn't succeed in getting me killed, so getting me out of town is the next best thing.

Which leads me to number five—I need to be wary of anything he suggests. However, getting David released is my first priority. I'll pretend to do whatever he says to protect David. Once he's released, though, all bets are off. I want to know why Williams thinks I present such a threat. And to whom?

Number six—What part does Avery play in all this? That's the question, isn't it? Williams said Avery "had feelings for me." Obviously, he didn't think that was a good thing. Is that why Williams wants me gone? Am I upsetting some kind of balance of power among the vamp bigwigs? If so, why didn't he just tell me? I could easily have put his mind at ease on that score. I'm not a political animal nor do I aspire to become one.

The sun is high in the sky. I glance at my watch. Noon. I have no desire for food, but a little company would be nice and I need to get a phone book to arrange for a security detail. I don't want any more little pricks pawing through my stuff.

I head for that bar down the block and get my usual table on the deck. Jorge smiles and welcomes me back.

This time my order is even simpler than before. Just a beer. *Erdinger* dark.

And a phone book.

He brings a frosty mug, a bottle, and the telephone directory. I open the yellow pages, pick a company in the beach area and make the necessary arrangements. When I'm assured a guard will be dispatched within the hour, I return my cell phone to my purse and turn my attention to the beer.

I pour and sip and let my eyes wander over the crowd on the beach. There's a party going on to the left. A lot of tight bodies playing sand volleyball to the right. And in front, a couple sunning themselves on a blanket.

I watch them, trying to remember how it felt to spend an afternoon with nothing more important on my mind than when to reapply sun block.

I envy them.

And as if picking up on my thought, the guy hoists himself into a sitting position and reaches for the Coppertone. He says something to his partner, and she rolls onto her side and takes the tube. He turns and she begins smoothing the lotion over a well-muscled back. Then it's her turn, and as he goes to work on her, his face is in my line of sight.

I almost drop the mug. I catch it before it makes too much of a mess, but a frothy wave of beer does manage to spill onto the tabletop and down my pant legs.

I hardly notice because I'm staring at the cop who stopped me for "speeding" the other night. One of the Revengers.

And at the same moment I recognize him, he sees me, too.

His eyes widen, and his hand stops in midstroke. We remain that way for what seems a long time, though I'm sure it's only a heartbeat or two. It's as if we're each waiting for the other to make a move.

He blinks first. He mumbles something to his companion and reaches for a cell phone. She doesn't turn to look at me, though, so I'm guessing he doesn't mention the fact that he's just spotted a vampire. Instead she starts gathering their things together, frowning as though irritated that their day at the beach has been disturbed.

I'm not irritated, though. I leave Jorge a ten and duck back inside the bar, watching through the tinted glass as the couple make their way to the street. Then I make a dash for my own car. It's only half a block down the road, and I move so fast I know they haven't seen me. In fact, the guy keeps looking back over his shoulder, completely unaware that I'm already in my car with the engine running, prepared to follow them. He's looking for a Jag, not an Explorer.

It's the break I've been waiting for.

CHAPTER 27

THE COP IS DRIVING A RED CORVETTE. MAKES IT really easy to tail. He leaves the beach and heads to Pacific Coast Highway. He jumps on I-8 and then switches to 163 near Mission Valley. He keeps going north, and I'm right behind him, though he doesn't know it. I can see him checking the rearview mirror, but he's still looking for the Jag.

He turns off at Genesee, the Linda Vista area, and makes a couple of quick right turns. We're in a housing area now and I have to be more careful. He, on the other hand, seems to have relaxed his guard. He takes no evasive action, but pulls right up into the driveway of a modest two-story bungalow on a street with the sweet name, Finch Lane. He doesn't even pause to look up and down the street, but he and his companion take their time unloading beach stuff from the back. I can tell from her expression and body language, she's still not happy that their afternoon was interrupted. He makes conciliatory gestures as they disappear inside the house.

I park a few doors down and wait. I'm betting he'll be back out in fifteen minutes tops—the time it takes to shower and change. What I'm hoping is that the telephone call he made on the beach was to his friends on the old Revenger squad. Probably made plans to meet them. I'm sure he thinks I ran when I recognized him.

Won't he be surprised!

He beats my time by a good five minutes. His hair is still wet and brushed straight back, as if he didn't want to take the time to dry it. He's dressed in jeans and a tee shirt, tucked, black leather boots on his feet. That's all. No gun that I can see, and even an ankle holster would show in jeans that tight. He jumps into the Corvette, fires it up and backs out of the driveway.

I make my move just before he leaves the neighborhood. At a stop sign, I let the Explorer roll into the Vette, a bumper kiss, but it gets his attention, as I knew it would. Corvette owners are touchy about their cars. Must have something to do with fiberglass.

In a flash, he's out of the car and scoping out the "damage." He's practically foaming at the mouth, he's so angry. By the time he gets around to aiming some of that fury at me, I've retrieved my gun and cuffs from the glove compartment. He still hasn't bothered to find out who's sitting behind the wheel of the Explorer, but I see him reach into his pocket.

He starts toward me, flipping open a leather wallet to reveal his badge.

I'm out of the door before he gets to the bumper of

my car. I'm holding the gun at my side. It's not until I'm right in his face that he realizes whose face is staring back at him.

His expression is almost comical. His mouth drops open, and his eyes widen.

I raise the gun slightly. "Get into my car, asshole, or I'll shoot you right here."

He looks around, gauging the possibilities.

"Don't even try it," I say. "I'm faster than you, stronger than you, and, oh yeah, I have a gun. Limits your options, wouldn't you say?"

He draws a breath and blows it out. "What about my car?"

"It'll be just fine here. If not, I'm sure the neighborhood tow guys will take good care of it."

He winces, but doesn't argue. I reach for his wallet and shove it into my back pocket. Never know when a badge might come in handy. He crosses in front of the Explorer and opens the passenger side door. He climbs in and I snap the cuffs around both wrists, through the armrest. If he tries to jump out, I can always drag him to death.

He doesn't say another word.

I pull the Explorer around the Corvette and park just on the other side of the intersection. It's a quiet neighborhood, but if I leave his car, it won't be long before someone notices a driverless Corvette at the stop sign.

"Don't move."

He rattles the cuffs. "Like I have much choice."

I jump out and get behind the wheel of his car. I'm really tempted to smash it into a tree, but it's not the car I'm angry with. Lucky for him.

After I've pulled it off the road, I toss the keys into a bush. When I rejoin him, he's frowning.

"Why'd you do that?"

"Because I felt like it. Any more questions?"

His lips press into a thin line.

"I'll take that as a no."

Up to this point, I've been reacting on instinct. Now it dawns on me that I don't know where to take this guy. I know *what* I want to do when I get him alone, but where to take him for privacy on a sunny summer afternoon is the question. His favorite haunt, the park, is out. That's probably where he was planning to meet his friends. He'd deny it, of course, so I won't waste my time asking.

Then I have it. Might be a little tricky, maneuvering a handcuffed man down a set of steep, slippery stairs. But we'd be alone, that's for sure. I head the Explorer back to the coast.

I must have a little smile on my face because he asks, "What's going on? Where are we going? You won't get away with this, you know. I'm a cop. My friends will come looking for me."

I almost hope they do.

Wait. I have to say it out loud for the jerk to hear. Vampire conversation is so much easier.

"The more the merrier."

He's squirming on the seat. "Look. It's not my fault what happened the other night."

"Oh, really? I could have sworn it was you who delivered me to your buddies."

"It's a job. Nothing personal."

That actually makes me laugh out loud. "Dying is personal. Even to the undead."

"You're not human. You feed on innocent victims. You don't deserve to live. You and your kind are freaks."

Sounds very much like what I said to Avery not too long ago. Funny, how one's perspective can change. "I don't feed on innocent victims," I say staunchly. "I've *never* fed on an innocent victim."

'Course, I've never fed on anyone except Avery, but I keep that to myself.

"You have to. Otherwise, you couldn't survive. It's what a vampire does."

"Where do you people get this stuff?"

Avery would be proud of the outrage I put in my voice.

He looks at me as if I'm speaking in tongues. "You are kidding, right? You really aren't going to tell me that vampires have gotten a bad rap over the ages? That it's all been a horrible misunderstanding? That Donaldson's victims deserved what they got?"

Donaldson. He would bring up that creep. I flounder a bit for the proper retort. All I can manage is a weak, "Donaldson was a rogue."

"*Was* a rogue?"

He picked up on that fast enough.

I nod. "He won't cause any more trouble."

He sits back in the seat with a satisfied smile. "Son of a bitch. They got him."

"Who's *they?*"

He directs that satisfied smile to me. "You'll find out soon enough."

But I want to find out now. We've arrived at our destination, and I reach into my pocket for my passenger's wallet. It's about time I found out this guy's name. I flip it open while he looks on, a puzzled frown on his face.

"What are you going to do with that?"

I smile. "Well, Trooper Lawson, we're going to take a walk. If we meet anyone, I'm an investigator bringing a suspect to the scene of his crime. If you try to get away, I'll simply flash this badge and shoot you. By the time it gets sorted out, I'll be gone. Are we clear?"

Lawson looks around. "We're at the Cove. What are we doing here?"

I've reached across him to pull my holster out of the glove box. When I'm properly attired, I hang his badge from my belt. "Looks good, doesn't it? Official."

He doesn't agree with me, not that I expect him to. I climb out of the Explorer and come around to his side. The good thing about dealing with someone who knows about vampires is that they understand the super human strength thing. He doesn't try to pull away when I uncuff him from the armrest and torque his arms around his back. When he's out of the car, I shove him against the door and do a thorough pat down. I know he isn't wearing an ankle holster, but he could have a knife tucked away in those boots. No sense taking chances.

I pull a thin, steel blade from a pocket in the lining of the boot. I hold it up. "Very nice. Wouldn't slow *me* down very much, but effective against humans, I suppose."

"I didn't know I'd be running into a vampire today."

I toss it into the car and nudge him forward. "I suppose not. If you had, you'd have shoved a stake down your pants, right? Let's go."

We're in the parking lot of an abandoned seashell shop right at the busy La Jolla Cove. There's yellow tape all around because of construction work. The old-fashioned shell shop is being remodeled into a new-fashioned gift shop. But anyone seeing a police officer escorting a handcuffed man through the back would probably assume it was crime scene tape. And since the crew seems to have left for lunch, it's easy for us to slip inside.

Lawson starts looking a little nervous when he realizes where we're going. "You're taking me into the cave?"

"Not as picturesque as where you took me," I reply. "But just as private."

The cave is a well-known feature of La Jolla Cove. To get to it, you have to take a flight of sheer, slick, stone steps straight down to the water. It's reputed to be an old pirate's hideout, and it's a good one. From land, you can't tell it's there. And from the sea, if you don't know what to look for, you'd never guess it was anything but sea-battered coastline. When the shell shop was open, it was a big attraction for tourists. Risk your life to see where a pirate stashed his booty. Deserted now, it's perfect for us.

Lawson stumbles on the wet steps. I don't help him. I let him fall to his knees, actually hoping he'll tumble all the way down to the water.

Soften him up a little.

He looks back at me as he struggles to his feet. "You could help me, you know. Take the cuffs off so I can use the rail."

"And miss the show? I don't think so. Keep going."

He mumbles something that sounds like "miserable vamp bitch" but I don't ask him to repeat it.

It takes a good ten minutes to get down to the water's edge. At the bottom, there's a little beach protected by a natural sea wall. The waves crash and boom around us, perfect insulation in case Lawson needs to yell or scream—or something.

He stops at the water's edge and turns toward me. "Well, we made it. What happens now?"

I look around for a place to stow the gun. Wouldn't want it to get wet. I find a little shelf in the rock and place it and Lawson's badge out of reach of the breaking waves.

Then I turn, too, and we're face to face. The cave throws jagged shadows, alternating light and dark, making him look like the jester on a pack of playing cards. He's scowling, holding himself upright, full of stubborn resolve.

But there's another vampire trait I'm starting to develop.

The ability to smell fear.

And right now, he reeks of it.

CHAPTER 28

O KAY, LAWSON," I SAY. "LET'S MAKE THIS EASY. You know what I want from you. You may as well give it up now and you'll live to fight vampires another day. If you don't, I may just rethink that feeding off innocent victims thing and give it a try."

He's still pulling a "you don't scare me" thing, still scowling, still stiff. "I don't have any idea what you're talking about."

"Okay. Then I'll give you a hint. He's about six foot six, weighs 250 pounds, broad shoulders, built like a tight end, which, oh yeah, he was. It's not going to go over very well when it comes out that a well-known football jock was kidnapped by a bunch of state troopers hunting vampires. Might even be the end of your career and the beginning of an all expense paid vacation to one of our more secure state institutions."

His face says I'm not going to tell you a thing, but his

shoulders are starting to slump a little. He puts steel in his voice when he says, "If you're talking about that partner of yours, what makes you think we had anything to do with his disappearance?"

I let a little smile touch my mouth. "Well, for one thing, you know he's my partner. And for another, you know he's disappeared, a thing I've only told two people, both of whom I trust a hell of a lot more than I trust you. So, I'll ask you once more in a nice way. Where is he?"

Lawson may be softening a little, but not enough to be convinced that I'm a real threat. I see it in his eyes. Maybe I need to be a little more forceful.

I've never done this before, but I decide it's time to see how my vampire face affects him. I'm not even sure how it's done, since with Donaldson it was more of an instinctive self-preservation thing. So I think about all that's been done to me in the last few days, the fire and the attacks on my life, and how David has been drawn into this through no fault of his own and how this asshole has the answers I need and I feel the change begin.

I watch it through Lawson's eyes. He shrinks back as if it's no longer a human he's confronting, but an animal. I hear a snarl, and realize it's from me. I feel my hands ball into fists and my lips curl back. My blood sings in my veins and a hunger for him becomes an overwhelming force that swallows what little humanity is left. Suddenly I'm not sure I can control what's happening. I'm drawn to him, my eyes on his throat because the pulse beating there becomes the center of my universe. Nothing matters but that I drink.

"Stop, please."

It's too late. I'm on him, ripping at the neck of his tee shirt, all that stands between me and the source of life.

He struggles back, falls. I'm on top. Teeth snap at the air, come closer.

"Please. I'll tell you. I know where he is."

Anna, stop.

My little voice is back.

I shake my head. *No.*

Lawson is screaming now, trying to twist away. I have his shoulders locked in my grip.

You have to. He knows.

I can't.

Yes. You can. Think. It's David's life.

A groan escapes my lips. *This is too hard.*

This is the way it is.

I push myself off Lawson and roll over onto my back. Every cell in my body is in revolt. The struggle to come back takes all my strength. I feel Lawson gasping beside me. If I still breathed air, I would be gasping, too. As it is, all I can do is lie very still and wait until I know it's safe. Until I know the human Anna is back.

It takes a while. Still, I recover before Lawson. When I pull myself into a sitting position and look over at him, he's heaving quietly into the water. There's a long, bloody gash on his cheek.

I move away. The scent and sight of blood threatens my resolve even now. I wait and watch as he pulls himself together, wipes tears and snot off his face, and hoists himself to his feet. His legs tremble and threaten to collapse under him. I don't dare lend a hand. It's too soon. All I can see is the ribbon of blood on his face.

Finally, his breathing returns to normal; color floods his cheeks. He braces himself against the rocks. When his eyes find mine, there's no fight left.

"Where is he?" I ask quietly.

He actually attempts a smile, though the effect is more of a grimace. "You must have really pissed somebody off," he says. "We're supposed to report when we spot you, but that's it. That's what I was going to do when you grabbed me. I swear, until today I had no idea you were connected to the kidnapping."

"Where is he?"

Lawson draws in a breath. "He's being held at some doctor's place," he says. "I don't know where exactly. But a vamp with a lot of pull warned us to stay out of it."

"A vamp warned you to stay out of it? I thought hunting vampires was what you Revengers were all about?"

He shrugs. "We have confidential informants in the vampire community who help us when it's in their best interest."

Their best interest? I snort. "You mean, they help you in return for not getting staked?"

He shrugs again.

"Let's get back to that doctor. Why would a doctor kidnap David?"

Lawson says, "Word was that some newbie irritated an old soul and was being punished. I figured it was somebody's boyfriend or husband—some kind of freaky love triangle."

"Then why did you say you were supposed to report if you saw me?"

He shakes his head. "Because that's what we were

told. I suppose it was because you got away from us. There were four sorry asses that got reamed because of that, mine included. I don't think the people in charge wanted that to happen again."

"And who are these 'people in charge'?"

Lawson debates what he's afraid of most—a pissed-off vampire or a pissed-off human. I see it all taking place on his face. He makes the right decision.

"There's a sergeant in our command. I don't know who he answers to. We just let him know when we've spotted a vamp and he mobilizes the team."

"Like the other night?"

He nods. "Just lucked into that one." He pauses, eyeing me. "Or maybe not."

"Let's get back to that doctor. You must have heard something else. Where does he live?"

"North County, I think. Or maybe La Jolla. Where do most doctor's live?"

Wide playing field and a whole lot of doctors. North County covers a lot of territory.

I turn away from Lawson and retreat a little into the shadows to think. Donaldson was telling me the truth in *Beso de la Muerte*. The fire and David's kidnapping had nothing to do with him. So why was he killed?

I turn my face back to Lawson. "You guys have an international chapter in Mexico?"

"What?"

"That's where Donaldson was killed."

He looks supremely ambivalent. "Could be. We only know the other three members of our team. That way, if we're caught, we can't give up anyone else."

Seeing how Lawson cracked under the proper persuasion, that makes sense.

"Of course," he continues, "it could have been a family member of one of his victims."

"Who knew he was a vampire and where to find him? How likely is that?"

He looks at me for a moment. "How long have you been a vampire anyway?"

"What kind of question is that?"

Something seems to dawn on Lawson. "Not very long, I'd say. First, you let me get you into the squad car without a fight. Now you're asking questions only a novice would ask."

A novice? It's that obvious? "I know enough about being a vampire," I say menacingly, "to know what to do with an insolent neck when I see one."

But that gets a smirk. "You should have told me the other night. Maybe I would have cut you some slack." He tilts his head as though trying to bring something to mind. "I know who you are. You're the one Donaldson let get away. You must be."

They know about that, too? "Where do you get your information?"

"I told you, confidential informants."

"And how would the family of one of Donaldson's victims know that he was a vampire?"

"Anybody can find out anything for the right price."

"From whom?"

"If you want something bad enough, there's always a way."

I reach over and thump his head. "Any more platitudes

rolling around in there or are you ready to give me a straight answer?"

He winces but stands his ground, finally saying, "There are people out there who deal in information like some deal in drugs. I can't give you a name."

None of this helps David. Impatience is quickly morphing into anger, my vampire temper rising. Lawson senses the change.

"I've told you all I know. Your partner was taken by a vamp doctor—"

"What?"

"A vamp doctor. I told you. I don't know why or where he's being held."

My heart starts pounding. "You didn't say it was a *vamp* doctor who took David. You just said it was a doctor."

He shakes his head. "No. I'm sure I told you it was a vamp doctor. A bigwig—"

But I don't hear another word he says.

I DECIDE TO SAVE TIME BY RELEASING LAWSON right outside the seashell shop. I uncuff him as we get to the top of the stairs.

The construction crew is starting to wander back from lunch, and we get a few strange looks as we appear from the cave.

Especially Lawson, whose clothes are stained and torn from our tussle down below.

One of the hardhats glares at us. "Can't you folks read? No admittance. It's dangerous down there."

I flash the badge. "Official police business."

He grunts and moves away, mumbling, "More like monkey business from the looks of you two."

Lawson is rubbing at his wrists. "What about my wallet?"

But I've already slipped it back into my belt. "I think I'll keep this as a souvenir."

"How am I supposed to explain losing my badge?"

"I don't care."

He stares at me a minute, decides it's useless to argue, and starts to open the car door.

I cut behind him and slam it shut. "This is as far as you go."

He looks like he can't believe what I just said. "You're leaving me here? Like this?" He sweeps a hand down his ruined clothes. "How am I supposed to get home?"

He's right. I should at least help him get home. I fish the wallet back out of my pocket, take the currency and credit cards from it, and hold those out. "Here. I don't need these."

He snatches them out of my hand. "Thanks for nothing."

But his sarcasm is lost on me. I'm already in the Explorer and cranking it over. I lower the passenger side window and lean toward him. "One more thing. If you breathe a word of this, I'll come back for you."

This time he looks as if he believes me.

CHAPTER 29

A VAMP DOCTOR HAS DAVID.
Nothing else Lawson could have said rocks me like that one statement.

The implication is clear. My rational mind tells me that with all the vampires in San Diego, Avery may not be the only doctor.

But as far as I know, he's the only one who can connect David with me.

Why would Avery kidnap David? And if he did, is he also responsible for the fire?

None of this makes sense.

I glance at the clock on the dashboard. It's almost two in the afternoon. Avery said he'd be at the hospital until six. At least I'll have some time to search the house before he returns.

Avery.

My heart lies heavy in my chest. I thought we had a

bond. More than the sex and blood thing. He appeared to be helping me—first in finding Donaldson and then David. Otherwise, what was the point of *Beso de la Muerte*?

Unless he thought I'd be killed there, too.

Could I really have been so wrong about him?

The driveway is empty when I pull up. This time, I drive around back, to the garage area. It's a stone structure, like the house, with three heavy iron doors to mark parking pads. I press a remote in the Explorer and one of the doors glides up. I pull the car inside and close it behind me.

There's one other vehicle inside—a restored Thunderbird from the sixties. The top is down and the tuck and roll upholstery shines in the overhead light. I run a finger over the leather, wondering if someone who could so lovingly restore a beautiful automobile like this be monster enough to put me in this much pain.

I check the garage out quickly. There are no trapdoors leading underground, no hidden loft areas above. If David is somewhere on the premises, it's got to be in the house.

There's a covered portico leading from the garage to the back door. In case the housekeeper is still inside, I ring the bell. I think I remember Avery saying she only comes in the mornings and when no one answers, I let myself in.

It's so quiet. I find myself tiptoeing from one room to the other. On the ground floor, there's the kitchen, dining room, library, living room. I can't find any other outside doors except the ones that lead to the balcony and deck areas and the front door off the foyer. There's no basement door, either, in spite of his joke this morning about keeping servants down below to drain their blood.

With a sick feeling, I find myself questioning if it was a joke. I almost retch at the thought that I might have been drinking David's blood. But a stronger, more virulent feeling overtakes the nausea. If Avery fed me David's blood, I'll kill him.

I've only been in two rooms upstairs, Avery's bedroom and the guestroom where Avery put my things. There are four other bedrooms up here, all expensively furnished with antiques, all tastefully appointed with drapes and carpets in muted earth tones. None of them look as if they've been used recently. In fact, all the closets are bare, the drawers empty. It's like walking through a designer showcase. Even the pictures on the dressers are fake—pretty frames with dime store photographs.

It dawns on me that there's nothing personal in Avery's bedroom either. I guess after hundreds of years, there's nothing personal left.

Is that what I have to look forward to?

I shake off the maudlin flood threatening to drown me and keep looking. At each end of the long hall that separates the bedrooms, there's a door. The one on the left leads to a back stairway. I follow it down to the kitchen. Then return to try the other one. It leads *up*. Evidently there's an attic.

The door at the top of these stairs is locked. I'm filled with apprehension. I press my ear to the door, but there's no sound. I knock and call out, "David?"

Nothing.

I put my shoulder against the door and shove. There's a splintering of wood and the door gives way. As soon as I step inside, I'm greeted with an unfamiliar odor—one of must and decay. Even not having to draw breath doesn't keep me from gagging. It's a reflex. The atmosphere in the room is suffocating.

Cautiously, I look around, mouth open, trying to gauge the source of the smell. It seems to come from a wall of chests, stacked near the top of the gables. As I approach, the smell gets stronger. Each chest looks different, but the size is pretty much the same. A little bigger than an old fashioned steamer trunk. There are eight or nine, some made of wood with metal hinges rusted with age, some made of more modern materials with brass or plastic hinges.

The most modern looking of all is also the one nearest my grasp. It's a plain, wooden affair with shiny hinges. There's a picture painted on the top, a portrait of a girl with golden hair standing in a window. She looks about twenty and her smile is full of joy and youth. She has on an old fashioned jumper and her hair falls in luxuriant curls to her shoulders. The portrait is so lifelike, it could be a photograph instead of a painting.

Something compels me to open this trunk, to see what lies beneath such a charming picture. My hand shakes as I release the catch. Before I see it, I know what it is. It's more than the odor, it's the *feel* of death. There are photographs inside, daguerreotypes brown with age, a lock of hair, a scrap of clothing.

And human remains.

A desiccated corpse that must have been lying here for years. Suddenly, I know why Avery said what he did the other night.

In the union between vampire and mortal, it's the vampire that suffers.

He was speaking from personal experience. I've found Avery's heart. Here in this attic, three hundred years of mortal lovers lost while the vampire continues unchanged and untouched by anything save this realization.

But there's another realization that hits me, too.

Like a knife in the chest.

David is not here.

Lawson either misunderstood or lied about David's kidnapper being a vamp doctor.

And I've invaded Avery's privacy in a way I know he'll never forgive.

I don't know what to do. I retreat from the attic mausoleum, softly closing the ruined door behind me. Avery will know at a glance that someone has been here. The idea that he lives with the mortal remains of those he's loved should repulse me. Instead, I'm filled with sadness and foreboding. Sadness because he clings to all that's left of love lost, and foreboding because I'm afraid it reflects something of my own future. I know now it's not a casket filled with earth from the mother country a vampire carries with him from one place to the other.

Seeking refuge in the guestroom, I stretch out on the bed to think. Avery is not due home for hours. I don't think I can wait that long. After a few moments, I find the paper he's given me with his hospital number and dial.

His receptionist answers, and when I tell her my name, I hear the smile in her voice.

"He's on his way home, Anna. He said he had a guest waiting for him. I must tell you, you've certainly put a spring in his step. He's not the same man he was a week ago."

I put the receiver down softly. And he won't be the same man tomorrow, either.

CHAPTER 30

I'M DOWNSTAIRS IN THE LIVING ROOM WHEN I hear Avery's car pull up. He drives around to the back, the same way I did, so I meet him at the kitchen door.

He smiles when he sees me, but the smile quickly fades. "What's wrong? Things didn't go well with Williams?"

Williams. I'd forgotten about him. So much happened after.

It's easier to let him pick the story out of my brain than to try to recount it. I "tell" him everything, right up until the time Lawson's story about a vamp doctor kidnapping David sends my world into a tailspin.

He senses there's more. *What aren't you telling me?*

I take him by the hand and lead him into the living room. I know I need to sit down for the rest of it. I imagine he will, too, after I've told him what I've done.

We take seats on the couch. I purposely leave distance between us. "I thought you were the one."

Confusion draws his brows together, pulls at the corners of his mouth. "The one?"

It takes him only a minute to understand. Then a dark, implacable expression settles on his face. "You thought I kidnapped David? Why on earth would you think that?"

"Lawson. He told me a vamp doctor had David. That he was taken to punish a newbie—for what, he didn't know. But suddenly all I could think of was you and I. You're a doctor, I've just become a vampire. It all fit. I just couldn't figure out why you'd want to do it."

Avery is very quiet. His thoughts shut off from me. But it takes no effort to interpret the emotions playing across his face. There's disbelief and the beginning of anger.

"How could you think I'd do something like that to you?"

I hold up a hand. *Avery, there's more.*

He grows very still, his eyes boring into mine as I let him learn the rest. I hope by doing it this way, he'll feel the shame and regret as well as hear the words.

But there's no way I can predict the depth of his rage as he learns how I violated his most inner sanctum. A wave of furious energy propels me against the arm of the couch as he leaps to his feet. He moves so fast, it's like watching a wisp of smoke blown out of the room by a turbulent gust of air. I hear thunderous footsteps on the back stairs and the grinding of broken wood as he wrenches open the attic door. Then there's silence, profound and terrible.

And I'm left alone and afraid.

CHAPTER 31

T HE SILENCE STRETCHES ON. TEN MINUTES. Then fifteen, and twenty. When I can no longer stand the wait, I force myself up the stairs. Avery is standing at the window, his back to me.

I'm sorry. It's all I can think to say.

He doesn't answer. Doesn't move. His mind is a black void, empty and cold. I've never felt anything like it. Even the temperature in the room has fallen. I find myself shivering, despite the bright sun, and know it's Avery who is doing it.

I have only one excuse, I begin again. *I was desperate to help David. He is my friend, and I must try to save him. Williams offered nothing but the possibility that he might be able to make some kind of deal with the Revengers. When I saw Lawson on the beach, I thought I might be able to make my own deal. What Lawson told me—*

Avery's voice cuts in, quiet and controlled. *You be-lieved I kidnapped David. You came here and searched my house and broke into a sacred place without first coming to me. You did all this despite what's happened between us.*

His back is still to me, and despite the dark energy emanating from him, the need to be closer compels me forward. I stand beside him, so close we almost touch, but unbidden, I can't take the chance to reach out.

That's a wise decision, he tells me.

Avery. You must understand my position. You've been a wonderful teacher. I don't think I would have survived the changes without you. But David is my best friend. I can't let him die without a fight. I won't. You talk about our natures. It's not in mine to abandon him.

I feel Avery move before my eyes register it. One moment he's next to me at the window, the next he's across the room, one hand resting on the casket of the young girl.

"This was my wife, Marianna." His tone is weary, his voice sounds ageless and old. "We met when she was a girl in the early nineteen hundreds. I didn't want to fall in love with her. Her father was a patient at the hospital where I practiced. He had tuberculosis, a death sentence in those days. His wife had already succumbed to the disease and there was nothing I could do to help save render him comfortable and free of pain. He knew he was dying. He begged me to look after his daughter because she had no one else and I agreed. When I saw her for the first time, at his funeral, I knew I was lost."

His fingers trace the delicate lines of the portrait. "She was so beautiful. Pure of heart and spirit. It had been a long time since I allowed myself to form an attachment to a mortal. I was more vulnerable than she. Still, despite my apprehension, I let myself fall in love. It was glorious at first. It was glorious until she learned of my 'nature.' She was twenty-five when she killed herself."

His eyes, clouded with visions of the past, clear and darken dangerously when he fixes them on me. *Don't speak to me of "nature," Anna. You have no idea what lies in store for you. The sooner you learn to separate yourself from the affairs of mortals, the better it will be.*

I don't understand you, Avery. You certainly have not separated yourself from mortals—you're a doctor.

He waves a dismissive hand. *My vain attempt to make amends for a hundred years of indiscretions. It took me that long to realize I wanted to live in harmony with men, not prey on them. Becoming a doctor enables me to do that without becoming involved.*

But there are caskets here to attest to the fact that you didn't always feel that way. You've fallen in love with mortals again and again.

"To my eternal regret," he thunders.

The sound of his voice makes me jump. "I'll probably feel the same way in a hundred years," I say quietly. "But first, I have a friend who has been missing for twenty-four hours. If you can't or won't help me anymore, I understand. But I'll find David, and if there is a vampire involved in his disappearance, he'll regret it, I promise you."

So now you think Williams is involved. He's picked it out of my head before I realize I'm actually thinking it.

Yes. He's the only other person who knows of our connection. I think you should know what he told me today. All of it.

I let him sort through the things Williams said. When I recall his comments about Avery wanting me gone, he stiffens.

"I never told him I wanted you to leave."

"Well, there's obviously a reason he wants me out of the way. Do you have any idea what that might be?"

Avery considers the question, leaving his mind open to allow me to follow his probe. But he shakes his head after a moment.

There is nothing in your becoming a vampire to threaten Williams. He is an old soul. Almost as old as I am. You are mistaken about him.

No.

I've taken a step back from Avery. *I may not know everything about him, but there's something not right about Williams. He lied to me about your feelings, for one thing. If it's true I don't threaten him in any way, why does he want me to believe you think I would be better off gone? It's the one argument he could make that might convince me.*

I've already told you, Avery counters stiffly. *I never said I wanted you to leave.*

Then what is it? What is it about me that threatens him?

Avery moves toward the door. *I don't want to stay in this room any longer. I'm going back downstairs.*

He waits for me to pass by him, pulling the door shut behind us, before he adds, *Any questions you have for Williams, you can ask him yourself. He'll be here in thirty minutes.*

IT'S A LONG THIRTY MINUTES. AVERY DISAPPEARS into the library, leaving me to wait in the living room with nothing but my thoughts. I've exhausted all of my options. Donaldson is dead, Lawson says the Revengers had nothing to do with David's kidnapping, and I seem to have alienated my best and only ally, Avery. Will he allow me to go after Williams? Or will he stop me from doing what I know I must?

When the doorbell rings and Avery doesn't appear to answer it, I go myself to the door. Williams is dressed as he was this morning, even has another cigar in his hand. He seems surprised to see me.

"I expected Avery."

"Why?" I counter. "You were supposed to call me, remember?"

He shrugs and pushes by me. "Is he here?"

"Does it make a difference?"

He tries to get into my head, but I don't let him. And I know he can't sense Avery's presence; house "security" would prevent that.

Very well. It's probably better if we speak in private anyway.

He leads the way to the living room. With the air of someone very much at home, he crosses to the sideboard opposite the fireplace and reaches underneath for glasses and a decanter. He raises a glass in my direction. "Would you care for a drink?"

I shake my head and watch as he pours himself a healthy two fingers. Even at this distance, I can tell what it is by the rich, oak smell. Scotch.

Williams takes a sip and smiles approvingly. *Avery always has the best.*

He seats himself on the couch, crosses one leg over the other and looks at me. *Are you going to sit down or do you plan to hover over me all evening?*

I don't plan to do anything with you all evening. Tell me what you've learned.

A little wrinkle of impatience creases his brow. *You really must learn to slow down. If you're lucky, you'll live a very, very long time. However, if you insist on rushing full speed ahead toward every little problem that presents itself, well, I'm afraid that may prove to be your undoing.*

Little problem? I've taken a step toward him. Outrage exudes like sweat from every pore of my body. It's overwhelming, this blind fury, and it scares me.

Williams, however, seems unaffected and certainly unafraid. The only reaction to my exhibition of temper is a raised eyebrow. *See what I mean? You'll burn yourself out if you continue this way. I've seen it happen.*

He's toying with me.

I know it. I should be able to deal with it. But too much has happened to me in the last few days, too many mental and physical changes with no chance to adapt. All the anger, frustration and fear boil to the surface. One moment I'm human, the next, animal. With no thought except that I want to wipe that smug look off Williams' face, I lunge at him, teeth and nails bared.

The ferocity of the attack knocks him off balance. He is not prepared for such a physical reaction. The glass flies from his hand, and his arms go up to shield his face. But he is older and stronger and when the shock of the unexpected wears off, he begins to fight back.

I know at once I can't win against him. Unlike Donaldson, he is a skilled fighter. He flips me onto my back and I'm pinned under him like an insect on the head of a pin. His lips roll back to expose sharp teeth, one hand is at my jugular.

What did I tell you? he hisses into my head. *Impatience will be your undoing.*

I look into his eyes. He will kill me, *wants* to kill me, and I am powerless to save myself.

I close my eyes, lift my chin to proffer the pulsing artery like a gift. I want it over. I can't save David. I can't save myself.

Suddenly, I just want it over.

CHAPTER 32

WILLIAMS' TEETH ARE AT MY NECK. HE'S snarling and snapping at me, coming closer and pulling away as if wanting to prolong my fear. Smiling as he enjoys the taste of it.

The smile is what pulls me back. It releases the hold he has on my mind. I can't, I won't let him kill me. In a last desperate effort to save myself, I gather strength to push against him. But his power is inexorable and relentless. He is an old soul. I understand in a flash that it is centuries of consuming the most essential of all life force—living blood—that gives him this capability. It is what he will use, finally, to kill me.

Unless.

I have Avery's blood coursing through my veins, don't I?

He is a most powerful vampire, older even than

Williams. He is the only creature I have fed from. Can I channel his energy for my own use?

I let my body relax for a moment, clear all thoughts out of my head.

Williams senses a change, pulls back a little as if to watch. His eyes narrow, his face feral and dangerous. Then he lunges again, and my instinct tells me he's tired of this game. He's ready for the kill.

But I'm ready, too. My blood is on fire now, my thoughts centered. I parry his thrust, get an arm between his face and my neck and push.

He flies off me and crashes into the coffee table. The splintering of wood and breaking of glass is lost in the howl of rage that escapes his lips. He pulls himself upright, all vestiges of humanity gone. I'm facing the animal now, and for a split second, terror is all I have.

But I recover quickly. I remember how it was with Lawson, how the vampire can swallow up the human, and I let it happen. I face Williams if not as an equal, then as the more desperate. I have nothing to lose, no inhibition about attacking a mortal to hinder me the way it did with Lawson. This will be a fight to the death. I use that realization to propel me forward.

When our bodies hit, it's with the force of a head-on collision between two semis. I dig my heels in and push him backward, for the first time cognizant of the fact that I might be stronger. He fights against it, but I don't let up. I want him on the ground, beneath me, subject to the same fear I felt moments before. I let him read that in my mind, see the flash of understanding bloom in his eyes. He knows I can do it. He knows I've fed from Avery.

But there's no fear. Only a sense of betrayal and regret that's quickly swallowed up by angry resolve. He has more reason than ever to want me dead.

Why? I back him into the stone hearth of the fireplace. *Why do you want me dead?*

He tries to shake me off. When he can't, he snarls at me like a wild dog. *You are a threat.*

A threat to what?

He continues to fight against me, but I have my arm across his jugular and the pressure is beginning to take its toll. His eyes roll back, his mind becomes a black void.

I loosen my grip, shake his shoulders. *No. Stay with me. Tell me what I want to know.*

Williams' eyes clear, his gaze refocuses. *I can't help you.*

I shake him again. *What about David? Who has him?*

His mind closes. It triggers another flash of rage deep inside me. I throw him onto the rug, pin him as he did me. But I don't tease. I rip into the soft skin at his jugular and drink.

An intoxicating, heady rush of explosive color and sound and emotion rips into me. Different from Avery, but the same. Not sexual, but basic. Williams' life experience, his memories, his history, are all there for the taking. And I do take it all. I let it flow into and through me. I crawl into his mind and nest there. I strain his thoughts like flour through a sifter until I find what I need to know.

Only then do I stop feeding.

He does not have David. He doesn't know who does. I pull back and shake his shoulders to get his attention. He has long since stopped fighting me. His mind is open, lethargic. I read something I don't expect. His acceptance of death. *You want me to finish it?*

He opens his eyes. *You are the stronger. Do what you will.*

Again, I'm caught off guard. *I don't understand. You have lived for centuries. You are ready now to die?*

I am ready to accept your will.

He speaks as if in prayer to a deity. Something in his tone, in his complete acquiescence rocks me. *Why do you say that?*

He reaches up a hand and grasps me behind the back of my neck, gently pulling me toward him. His voice is a whisper in my ear. *You have the power now. Finish it.*

I recoil as if hit, rearing back to search his face. *What do you mean?*

He nods, smiling, a sad, sweet smile. *Avery was right. You are the one.*

The one?

Ask him.

And then he's gone. It's like nothing I've experienced before. His mind closes utterly and completely, like the flatline when brain death occurs. His eyes are open and staring, his body rigid.

I open my mouth to scream and Avery is there.

CHAPTER 33

A VERY PULLS ME AWAY FROM WILLIAMS. *WHAT have you done?*

But there's no anger or rancor in his tone or on his face. I search his mind, find nothing I can read there, either. A wave of desolation sweeps over me. *I don't know.*

He gathers me against his chest, rocking me as he would a child. *It's all right.*

I want to burrow into Avery, let his strong arms protect me from a danger I can't even begin to understand. But I know it's not possible. The danger is within me. Reluctantly, I move away from him.

I don't know what happened.

Avery's eyes move from Williams' face to my own. *You didn't drain him?*

My eyes widen. It's a simple question but the implication that Avery knows I could have drained Williams surprises me. *No. He spoke to me. Just before . . .*

A stirring in Avery's mind, a subtle shift. *What did he say?*

He's guarding his thoughts, but this time in a different way. Not just to prevent me from reading them, but to protect something. Himself? From me?

He frowns. *Tell me, Anna. What did he say?*

Nothing that made sense. He told me I was "the one." That I had the power. He told me to ask you what that meant. And then he was gone. Avery, is he dead?

Avery moves to Williams, kneels beside the body, presses a hand to his chest. *He's not dead.*

Then what?

He's in stasis.

Stasis? What does that mean?

Avery passes a hand over his face as if suddenly weary. *It happens sometimes with us. A withdrawal from reality. It's a kind of suspended animation. Vampires do it when they're under severe pressure or when they feel death approach. He feared you would kill him.*

A shudder passes through me. I feared I would kill him, too. I wanted to. He doesn't know where David is or who has him, and yet, he would have lied if I hadn't taken the information.

I bring my eyes up to meet Avery's. He is watching me closely, a frown still pulling at the corners of his mouth. *He knew once you took what you needed, you would be finished with him. He thought you would kill him. This is the way he protected himself.*

But I could have killed him anyway.

He took the risk that you had enough humanity left in you to prevent that. He was right, wasn't he?

Was he? I'm not sure.

I turn away from Avery, and Williams. I can't look at either of them.

How long will he be like this?

I feel Avery come close. His hands touch my shoulders. When he speaks, it's a whisper in my ear.

"There's no way of telling. It could be hours. It could be days or weeks."

"What do we do with him then? What do we tell his wife?"

Avery turns me to face him. *She will be told the truth. Williams will have prepared her for this possibility. As for the rest of the world, Chief Williams will have suffered a stroke. We have a facility nearby where his needs will be met. He will be well cared for. You did nothing wrong. Now, I must make some telephone calls. Perhaps it would be better if you went upstairs. No one need know you were here.*

Reluctantly, I agree. There will be nothing to gain by complicating matters with my presence. The truth will not be known to anyone except Williams' wife, and even then, I'm sure what Avery tells her will be an altered version of what really happened. Again, I owe Avery my life. He always seems to have my best interest at heart.

I trudge up the stairs to my room. I stretch out on the bed, listening as an ambulance arrives, listening as voices drift up and away, listening as Avery recounts a story that is accepted as the truth because of who he is. Eventually, the voices quiet, the sirens move off, and Avery is at my side.

It's over now. You are safe.

But David is not.

Avery sits on the edge of the bed, draws me to him. *I'm sorry about David. But Williams was your last hope to find him. You must let it go now.*

Despair settles around me like a velvet curtain being drawn, thick and black and shutting out hope. Still, I shake my head, fighting it.

I don't understand this, I tell him. *Why was David taken? What sense does it make? I've gone over this a thousand times in my head. If it had been Donaldson or the Revengers, at least there's a connection there. They know I'm a vampire. But David knows nothing about what happened. He isn't a threat to anyone. I can't let it go until I find out what happened to him and why. I won't.*

Avery's arms drop away. Aggravation and impatience form a crease in his brow, though he fights to conceal it from his thoughts. Instead, the tone of his voice is patient and full of understanding.

"What do you think you can do now? You've exhausted all leads. There's no one left to help."

"Then I'll start over. I'll go back to *Beso de la Muerte.* I'll talk with Donaldson's vampire friends. Maybe I was wrong about him. Maybe David is there somewhere—"

"Do you really think he'd still be alive if he was?" Avery pushes himself to his feet. "You can't keep doing this. You have to accept that David is lost. You must learn to separate yourself from mortals. It's a lesson best learned at the beginning. It will save you centuries of heartache. One day you will look back at this and realize it was the best thing that could have happened to you."

Avery's agitation is like a knife thrust. He pounds one fist into the other as he paces. "It could have been worse," he continues. "Don't you realize it could have been your parents or Max that were taken? This is a warning. You are not like them anymore. You are immortal. You will watch your parents wither and die, and Max will be a vessel to draw from, nothing more. You don't need them anymore, Anna. You don't need anyone—"

But me.

Avery opens his mind and the frenzy of negative feeling is gone. Instead, his thoughts are full of love, overwhelming, complete. He's beside me on the bed, his look a question.

Confusion snarls my thoughts. I start to pull away, but his emotion is so intense, I'm swept along. I'm in his arms and I can't tell where his passion leaves off and mine begins.

I don't fight it. I don't want to. I don't understand what's happening, but he offers me the one thing I seem to find only in his arms—safety. I let him strip off my clothes, feel his hand sear a path down my abdomen, explore my thighs, move up. My own urgency soon matches his. This is much more than sexual desire and the degree to which I respond stuns me. I find myself calling his name over and over. And more.

Love, intense, relentless as a riptide permeates my being.

Can he feel it?

Do I want him to?

It's too late to wonder about it now. Imprisoned in a web of arousal, I let desire spiral through me until it soars to a height of passion I have never known before.

CHAPTER 34

I'T'S NOT UNTIL AVERY HAS LEFT MY BED THAT I start to think, something that does not seem possible when he's touching me. Did I let Avery know that I loved him? Did he read it in my thoughts? I don't even know if it's true, but it certainly felt like it at the time. And it certainly drove all other considerations from my head. Important things, like finding David, something I'm not ready to give up on.

If Avery was a witch, I'd think I was under a spell. But Avery is a vampire. We don't cast spells.

Do we?

I'm hovering on that point between consciousness and sleep when a flash of something important jolts me awake. It's something Williams said, something I should ask Avery about. It's that thing about being "the one." It all got lost in what happened to Williams and in what happened after that.

But I can ask him now.

I throw off the covers and shrug into the robe Avery left for me. He's gone into his own room to shower, and when I knock on his door and there's no answer, I let myself in anyway. I'll wait for him to finish.

But the bathroom door is open and I don't hear the shower running. I pad into the bathroom. Perhaps he's taking a bath. It was only a day or so ago when he walked in on me in the tub. Turnabout is certainly fair play.

But the shower is empty and dry, as is the bathtub. Did he go downstairs to get a drink? I start to send out a mental query to determine his whereabouts when I remember it won't work—that pesky white noise. I'll have to find him the old fashioned way.

It's dark and quiet in the house. My vampire night vision allows me to see without turning on lights, and I make my way downstairs and into the living room. The debris from the broken coffee table has been swept away. I suppose Avery took care of that before the ambulance arrived. There's not even a shard of broken glass to hint at the battle that took place here.

A tremble passes through me. I'm not ready to face what I did to Williams, because in spite of what Avery said, I know I'm to blame. Williams was so afraid of me, he willed himself into a state of suspended animation. I can't understand how a strong, old soul could be driven to such a thing by a newbie.

But I push the thought out of my head. I need to find Avery. Perhaps he can make sense out of the riddle Williams spun. I know I can't do it alone.

A search of the library and kitchen yields nothing.

Avery is not in any of the downstairs rooms, nor is he on the deck. Puzzled, I start back up the back stairs to the bedroom landing. As I get to the top, it hits me that perhaps Avery has gone to the attic. If he has, am I prepared to intrude? The intensity of his anger is rivaled only by the intensity of his passion. I've evoked both in him today.

I'm unsure what to do. I'm standing in the hall between our bedrooms when I hear it. The sound of a door opening. From inside Avery's room.

But I was just in there. The adjoining bathroom doors were already open and the closets are walk-ins. No doors. Yet I hear the distinct clatter as the tumbles of a lock click into place. Then Avery's footfalls pad across the carpet and the rush of water from the shower floats out across the still night air.

Uncertainty grips me. There's another door somewhere in Avery's room? Where does it go? Why didn't I see it when I was looking around this afternoon?

I feel rooted to the spot, unable to make a decision. After all that's happened today, I don't trust my instincts. One part of me wants to barge right in there and turn the room inside out until I find that secret door. The other, saner part keeps asking why I would do that. After all, this is a vampire's house—an old vampire's house. Perhaps the secret doorway leads to nothing more than a safe room where Avery keeps valuables or money. What right do I have to break into something like that? How would I explain it to the man I was just making love to? A man who has come to my rescue more than once in the last week. A man who can very probably tear my head right off my shoulders if I piss him off again.

So I take the line of least resistance and go on back to my room. After all, Avery is going to the hospital tomorrow morning. I can snoop all I want then.

AVERY WAKES ME UP WITH A KISS, HIS FINGERS busy down there, and once again, I'm swept away. When it's over and rational thought has returned, I ask him about Williams' comments.

He stretches and yawns and smiles down at me. *I think you must have been mistaken. I know nothing of anyone "being the one" or "having the power." It sounds melodramatic to me.*

But I shake my head. *No. It was in his blood. There was no mistake.*

Avery turns away from me, shaking off the covers as he gets to his feet. *I have to go. Early rounds.*

He leans down and brushes my forehead with his lips. *We'll talk more tonight. I want to take you to dinner. Someplace special. Are you up for that?*

I try to read what he has in mind, but nothing comes through. *Yes. I'd like that. But we do have to talk. David—*

But he brushes the air with his hand, and there's a flicker of annoyance at the corners of his mouth before he smoothes it away. *I have to go. I'll send a car for you at eight.*

I won't see you until then?

He throws me a secretive look. *I have some arrangements to make. I think it will be worth the wait.*

And then he's gone, sweeping from the room without a backward glance.

There's a subtle shift in his attitude this morning. A confidence that I am his. He has read it in my thoughts, after all. He has felt it in the way my body responds.

All too true.

Still, I burrow under the covers and wait for him to leave the house.

CHAPTER 35

WHEN I'M SURE AVERY IS GONE, WHEN I'VE watched his car disappear down the driveway from the window opposite my bed, I get up, shower, and pull on jeans and a tee shirt. I hear the housekeeper moving around the kitchen, so I know my time is limited. She'll come up to make the beds when she's through with her downstairs duties.

There is a battle waging inside me. The way I've come to trust Avery feels complete and right. Yet, the need to know all his secrets is overwhelming. I can't explain why. I just know I must.

I tiptoe into his room, lock the door behind me. I let my eyes run over everything—there are bookcases against two walls, a fireplace against another, windows on the fourth. The door into the bath faces the bed. The only logical place for a secret door would be behind those bookcases.

I run my hands over the shelves, peek behind books, drag a chair over so I can climb up and look over the top. Nothing jumps out at me; no outline of a door presents itself.

What now?

I step back and look again. What am I missing?

The doorknob on the outside door jiggles as someone tries it. Then there's a gentle tap.

"This is the maid, Miss. Shall I come back later?"

I blow out an exasperated sigh and cross to let her in. "Sorry," I say, swinging open the door.

She's not what I expect. She's young, twenties, maybe, and beautiful in an exotic way. Her shiny, black hair hangs straight to her shoulders framing a thin face with huge, dark eyes and a generous mouth. Hispanic/Asian mix, maybe, or Eurasian. She's dressed in jeans and a baggy tee shirt over which hangs a white linen apron. She looks embarrassed at having disturbed me.

I hold out my hand. "My name is Anna Strong. I'm a friend of Avery's." I smile. "But you knew that, didn't you?"

She returns the handshake timidly. "Dr. Avery said he had a guest. And that I wasn't to disturb you."

"You didn't. Really. I'll leave you to your work Miss—?"

"My name is Dena. And I can come back later."

She's so serious—almost deprecatingly so. Very different from the attitude of most twenty year olds. She almost seems afraid of me.

Why?

I wave a hand at her as I pass into the hall. "No. You do what you need to. I'll be downstairs, all right?"

She nods and turns away and it's then I notice two tiny marks on her neck. They are not fresh, but whoever made them didn't use his vampire power to heal them, either. I touch her shoulder and she jumps.

"I'm sorry. I didn't mean to startle you. I was curious, though. How long have you worked for Dr. Avery?"

Dena shrugs and, as if suddenly aware of what I've seen, tugs at the collar of her tee shirt. "Not long. I had an accident several months ago. I was a patient of Dr. Avery's and he was kind enough to offer me this position when I was released from the hospital. I needed a job. He lets me work in the mornings so I can go to school in the afternoons. He's been a godsend."

But her tone is less than convincing. And as she speaks, she backs away from me, twisting at the hem of her apron. She's not vampire. I'm sure of that because there's no path that I can find into her mind. But she's afraid of me because she recognizes that I am.

I smile at her gently, trying to ease her fear. "I'll leave you now, Dena."

Her eyes never leave my face. I feel them follow me as I make my way back to my own room. For the first time, I'm aware of a dark side to Avery. That in spite of all his talk about wanting to work with rather than prey on mortals, he has taken advantage of this girl. I know it as well as I know my new strength, as I know I am no longer human. As I know that she senses the difference. She may have offered herself at first, been excited or flattered that the handsome doctor showed such interest.

But she doesn't want it now. Is he still feeding from her? Was it her blood he offered me the morning I came back from *Beso de la Muerte*?

I'm filled with angry impatience as I wait for Dena to finish in Avery's room. I'm more determined than ever to find out what he's hiding. When we're together, it's truly as if I'm under his spell. He makes me forget everything except the touch of his hand, the taste of his blood. But I know very little about him—only what he wants me to know. And I've let him shape my knowledge of what it is to be vampire in his own image.

It's time I learn more. Maybe some of those secrets are hidden in this house.

Dena tiptoes past my room, anxious to be on her way, afraid that I might try to stop her. I hear it in her halting footsteps, see it in the drawn expression on her face as she passes my open door. I let her go, listening to the sounds of the front door closing, the clicking of the deadbolt, the cranking of a car engine. When I'm sure I'm alone, I head back for Avery's bedroom.

No finesse this time. I pull books out of the case, use vampire strength to move them from the wall, run my hands up and down to search for hidden seams.

Nothing.

Shit.

I slump down on the foot of the bed. I try to remember exactly what I heard last night. Avery moving from somewhere along this wall into the bathroom.

Or was it this wall?

I turn to the fireplace. There's a massive stone hearth with a raised platform in front and storage areas for wood on either side. The storage areas are both well over six feet tall and the one on the right is stacked floor to top with neatly sawed, fragrant logs of cedar and pine. The one on the left is only half full, though. And when I peer at it closely, a faint outline presents itself.

But if this is the door, how to get in? Avery certainly didn't have time to remove all these logs last night, then replace them when he came back. I heard the door close and he moved immediately away.

There must be a hidden catch.

I take a step closer. The mantel is a solid slab of heavy dark wood. I run my fingers over the surface, above and below, not knowing what I'm searching for, but not feeling anything that might activate a door either. Stepping back again, I look up at two big brass sconces on either side of the hearth. Could this be the way in?

I reach up for the one on the left. I tug, pull, twist.

Nothing.

I move to the opposite end. This time, when I pull there is a grinding sound, like a gear mechanism springing to life. I jump back and watch as the left side of the fireplace moves in on itself, the entire wall disappearing into a passage that stretches into a black void in front of me.

I've found the way into Avery's secret room.

I have to wait a moment, to let my eyes adjust from the bright sun-filled bedroom to the darkness of the passageway. When my vampire vision takes over, I take a step inside.

There's a long, wooden staircase that looks to descend

straight down, almost like a ladder. The staircase is narrow, not more than two feet wide. One wall is stone, the outside wall of the house probably, the other, wood. There is a handrail, which I grip tightly as I start down. I can't see to the bottom. I can't hear anything, either. There's an eerie stillness that sends an involuntary shiver up my spine.

There must be a hundred steps. When I touch ground I'm standing on a dirt floor. The musky smell of decaying vegetation tells me that I'm deep underground. Avery has built himself an earthen fortress.

I spot a door ahead of me about fifty feet from the bottom of the stairs. I know it won't be locked. Avery would not expect anyone to find this place without him. And I'm right. The door yields under my touch.

It's a large room, maybe twenty by thirty, stacked with wooden crates on one wall, shelving against another. There is a switch to the right of the door. I throw it and the room jumps into stark relief. The shelves are strewn with pieces of pottery, vases, items of gold and silver that glitter despite the gloom of a dim subterranean light—all that's needed with vampire vision.

I don't know much about art, but I recognize the magnificence of what I see in front me. The graceful beauty of ancient Chinese porcelains, the intricate scrollwork of Egyptian antiquities, the simple magnificence of Mayan pottery and jewelry—I've discovered the source of Avery's wealth. Accumulated across the centuries, I imagine, doled out piece by piece when the need arises. I can't tell what's in the crates, but I'd be willing to bet it's more of the same. The contents of this room could fill a small museum—or keep one immortal living in splendor forever.

There's nothing incriminating here, not really. Of course I have no way of knowing how he came by such treasure. Being vampire, I'm sure it might not be all on the up-and-up. But what great fortune, human or vampire, was ever accumulated without the hint of impropriety? I've found nothing to justify another invasion of Avery's privacy. I've once again thought the worst of him and been mistaken.

Casper was right. My instincts are certainly off. Well, at least I can make this right. I can keep Avery from finding out about my foray into his underground vault. It won't be easy keeping it out of my thoughts, but I will do it. I don't want to risk losing him because of another vague, unsubstantiated suspicion.

What I need to do now is focus, concentrate on finding David. I'm going to have to start all over. I'll leave for *Beso de la Muerte* tonight. Avery won't like it, but he'll have to accept it.

As I make my way across the floor toward the door, I notice for the first time that there is something else in the room. A bundle, deep in the shadows, that looks like a roll of carpet propped lengthwise against the third wall.

Probably an ancient Persian rug plucked from the castle of a king.

I hardly give it another glance—at first.

But then—

A tiny movement.

Did I imagine it?

Eyes riveted on the carpet, I find myself propelled toward it. Chilling, black silence envelops me.

I prepare myself for the worst.

I kneel down and peel back a corner, shaking so badly I have to grasp the rug with both hands.

I think I know. I think I'm ready.

But the horror of what I see is more terrible than anything I imagine.

I've found David.

Bound and gagged and lying still as death on that dirt floor.

CHAPTER 36

I HEAR A MOAN, DEEP AND FULL OF DESPAIR. IT takes me a moment to realize it's my own voice, my own despair. I'm still shaking. I can't even hold myself upright, but slump against David's side, my arms around him, my face pressed against his. How could this have happened? How could I have let this happen?

How could Avery do this to me?

It is at that moment that I feel it.

A slight movement in my arms, a turn of the head, a shallow intake of breath.

I fear it's my imagination. I pull back, put my ear to his chest. Listen.

A faint heartbeat.

He's not dead.

Ripping at the carpet, I pull it away, ease the constriction around his chest. He moans a little, but his eyes remain shut, his breathing labored. I hold his head in my hands and shake it gently from side to side.

"Come on, David. Open those beautiful eyes. Talk to me."

There's no response. He's deep in some sort of coma. Drug induced maybe. Or—

I move his head slightly. I find what I expect. Avery has fed from David.

There are two marks at his jugular. Not small pin-pricks like Dena's, but ugly, gaping wounds made by someone in a feeding frenzy. Someone not caring that he's leaving marks because he knows his victim will never be found.

Avery.

Anger, like a scalding iron, burns so deep in my gut I have to force it back and out of my thoughts. Revenge will come later. First and foremost, I must get David to safety. With a jolt, I realize I know nothing about how feeding affects the human physiology. Will David re-cover on his own? Does he need a transfusion? Can I risk taking him to a hospital?

I don't have the answer to any of those questions. The only person I could ask is the last person I can. Gathering David in my arms, I lift him like a doll and carry him up the stairs. I lay him out on Avery's bed and return to the room. Rolling the carpet back up, I prop it against the wall the way I found it. If Avery should re-turn while I'm gone, at first glance the room will look just as he left it.

Then I set about putting the bookcase in order. I have no idea how the books were arranged, stupid of me not to have noticed, but Avery is an organized man and I have to imagine he would sort his books by topic. I reshelve the medical books together, then fiction, then general nonfiction. If he asks about it, I'll tell him Dena was dusting in here and I interrupted her before she could finish so I put the books back myself.

Lame. But it's all I can come up with.

Besides, Avery will have more pressing problems to deal with than his disrupted bookcase.

Grimly, I take a last look around the room. The fireplace door is shut, the sconce back in its upright position. I lift David off the bed and take him downstairs and out the kitchen door to the garage. I lay him in the backseat of the Explorer, out of sight under a blanket, and then I realize I've left my purse and cell phone inside.

I'm almost to the back door when I hear a car coming up the driveway. Did Dena forget something when she was here earlier? I shade my eyes from the bright noonday sun and look toward the gate.

But it is not Dena's car approaching. It is Avery's.

My first impulse is to fly at him, to give him no chance to flee or fight back. To tear him apart for what he's done.

But I know I can't do that. At least, not yet. I need to get David help. And there are questions Avery needs to answer.

I gather myself together, calm the wild beating of my heart, obliterate all thoughts of what I've found this morning. He cannot know what I've done.

And so when I go to meet him, I'm smiling. And when he takes me in his arms to kiss me, I kiss him back.

He pulls away after a moment and waves a hand toward the garage. "Were you going out?"

"I was going shopping," I reply without hesitation. Lying seems to have become second nature. "I wanted to get something special for tonight."

He smiles and reaches into the backseat of his car. "I've saved you the trouble." He pulls a long, plastic dress bag from inside and holds it out to me. "I thought this would look lovely on you."

I move the zipper down a little, just enough to see the jeweled top of a designer gown, bright red with tiny straps and a label that reads Badgley Mischka. I look up at Avery. "One of New York's hottest designers. How did you manage that?"

"Not a problem, when you have the right friends," he replies, his eyes sparkling with pleasure.

I drape the bag over my arm. *Thank you. Are you coming in?*

Avery shakes his head. *I wish I could. But I have surgery all afternoon. I just wanted to give you the dress and remind you that I'll send a car for you at eight. We are going to have an evening you'll never forget.*

And at that moment, I almost lose it. I almost let him know just how right he is.

But he doesn't pick up on my disquiet, doesn't sense the rage. He's too full of his own pleasure, too self-satisfied. He kisses me again, gets back into his car and pulls away, waving at me and grinning, completely oblivious to the oncoming storm.

When Avery's car disappears from sight, I retrace my steps to the kitchen, where I retrieve my purse and phone and return to the garage. David hasn't moved. I make sure he's as comfortable as I can make him before I take the garment bag Avery left with me and lay it out in the area behind the backseat. I want to rip the damned thing to shreds, but I console myself with the thought that I'll do the next best thing. I'll be wearing it when I rip Avery to shreds.

But first—where do I take David? I consider and reject my parents' home, a motel, a hospital. I can't risk the possibility that Avery had me followed the day I went to La Mesa to retrieve my things, or that he's having me followed now. I don't think that's the case. He seems too sure of me. But he has so many contacts in so many places, any public venue might be a danger. And there are a lot of vampires out there, any one of whom might turn me in for a return favor.

Which leaves one other possibility. I can take David back to his own place. Anyone following would think I'm back on the trail. And if Avery returns and discovers David is gone, I doubt the first place he would think to look for him would be David's own place. Besides, Avery won't have the chance to get to him again. I plan to make sure of that.

And so I bring David home. It's quiet in the garage when I pull in. The guest spaces are close to the elevator, and since it's midday and most of the building's occupants are at work, I manage to get David out of the car and into the elevator without incident. I don't know how I would have explained a 125 pound woman carrying a 250 pound man like an oversized doll, but luckily,

I don't have to. No one else stops the elevator and we shoot right to the top floor.

I use David's keys to get inside. I lay him on the couch, retrieve a blanket and pillow from his bedroom, and try to make him as comfortable as I can. His breathing is still labored, but his heartbeat is strong. He's so pale, his skin looks translucent. The wound on the side of his neck is weeping and raw. I think back to what Avery said in his kitchen yesterday morning. *I drain just enough from them to sustain my own life and prolong theirs.*

If that's true, how long would it take for a mortal to recover from prolonged feeding? When you give blood, they tell you you must wait 56 days after donating a pint before you can donate again. How many pints has Avery drained from David if he's had him two days? Somehow, I don't think Avery used caution in his feeding. He planned to kill him.

I rub a hand over my face. I don't know what to do. The best thing would be to get David to a hospital where a transfusion could replace some of his lost blood. But I can't risk it. For all I know there are other doctors like Avery in every hospital who would pick up on David's condition the minute he got there. Once word got out, I might not be able to protect him.

And Avery has connections everywhere, isn't that what he said?

I glance at my watch. It's noon. I have only eight hours to decide what to do.

What else do they tell you when you donate blood? I used to do it quite often, though I imagine that's something else that stops now. Just what type is a vampire's blood?

I drop down beside David on the end of the couch. Think. They tell you to take it easy. A glance at David's motionless form—not a problem. They tell you to drink plenty of liquids, especially juice and water. A trip to David's refrigerator reveals plenty of both. I take a bottle of water and return, propping him up with an arm while I try to get him to drink. There's no reflex swallowing action, and the water dribbles down his shirt-front.

He's pale and so limp and still. I press my hand against his chest. The heartbeat seems steady, but for how long? I have to get him help.

I'm at the window, staring out at the bay, when a germ of an idea starts to bloom. It's crazy. Risky. Probably stupid.

But it's the only way I can think of to save my friend.

I'm going to take him to *Beso de la Muerte*.

CHAPTER 37

I DON'T WASTE ANY TIME DEBATING WITH MYSELF, even though Avery is the one who told me about the place. I remember the setup they had, the triage unit with gurneys and IV lines. If I can get David there, he might have a chance.

So, I gather David in my arms again, and it's back down to the garage. This time we're not so lucky. When the elevator door opens to the parking lot, there's a couple standing there whose expression at seeing us can only be described as startled. I breeze by them with a smile.

"Pretty lifelike for a blow-up doll, huh?"

I don't wait for a reply, but dump David rather unceremoniously into the backseat. The couple watches as I take my place behind the wheel and pull away. They remain watching until I'm out of the garage. But I don't see them reach for a cell phone, so I have to assume they aren't calling the police. Probably can't figure out how to explain what they saw without sounding completely crazy.

Once I'm down the road a bit, I pull over and tuck David away more comfortably, pulling a blanket up over his head, and covering him with the garment bag. Not too successful a camouflage job, but the best I can do. I make one more stop at my bank and drive through to cash a thousand-dollar check. I have no idea how much Culebra will charge me for services, but maybe this will do as a down payment.

Then I'm heading south on Interstate 5 and back toward the border.

The border crossing is busy at midday. It takes an hour, but once I get to the checkpoint, I get only a cursory nod and a wave from the guard in my lane. Another thirty minutes and I'm clear of TJ. I hit Highway 2 and speed toward *Beso de la Muerte*. There's more traffic during the day, but it thins as I approach the turnoff and dies completely once I've hit the dirt road that runs to town. I've made the decision to drive straight in, not carry David in my arms, to save time.

It's very quiet. The saloon looks deserted. There's no loud music, no sound of laughter or voices from within. I guess the residents keep a low profile during the day. I don't even slow down, but continue to the cave in back. I know my approach is being monitored; my vampire alarm is tingling. I can only hope I get a chance to explain why I'm here before someone tries to kill me.

There's a man waiting for me as I pull up at the cave entrance. It's the same man I saw speaking with Max's boss the first time I was here. He's also dressed the same as before—same worn jeans, same ragged poncho. Today, however, he has a straw sombrero on his head, and a pair of expensive Ray-Bans covers his eyes. Up close, he looks like a character out of a Sergio Leone western. His teeth are yellow, his nose crooked, the lines on his face etched deep as tire tracks. He's holding a crossbow in his hands and he raises it to my chest the minute I get out of the car.

Does he know I'm vampire?

A smile tweaks the corner of his mouth. "Not until you just told me," he says. He motions with the bow. "But this is an effective weapon against all intruders, mortal or not, wouldn't you say?" His accent is heavy, but his English is perfect.

And he's read my mind. Yet he's not vampire, I can feel it. *What are you?*

Again the smile. But no answer. And I can't penetrate his thoughts. Still, there's a reason I'm here and I let him read it for himself. All except the identity of the vampire who fed from David. He probably knows Avery.

He looks surprised as he picks through my thoughts. "You are concerned over the fate of a mortal?"

"He is my friend. I don't want him to die."

"And how do you think I can help?"

I let him know about my previous visit here.

He sweeps the glasses off his face and fixes me with a hard stare. Little pinpricks of light flash from ebony eyes. "Ah, yes. I remember the night you were here. The night Donaldson disappeared. I saw you in the trees."

An icy finger at the back of my neck. "I didn't kill him."

"But you wanted to. It was the reason you came, wasn't it?"

"Yes."

"At least you are honest. What do you have to offer in exchange for my helping your friend?"

I pull the wad of bills from my pocket. "I can get more."

He takes the bills, fans them in his hand, thrusts them back at me. "I will help you. But not for money. You will owe me a favor. Do you agree?"

I nod, wondering if I've just sold my soul to the devil.

"Not the devil," he replies. "But close, maybe."

He creeps me out with that, sends a shiver down my spine, but I shake it off. David is the important consideration here. Not me. I'm the reason he's dying.

"Bring your friend inside."

He waits as I lift David from the car and leads the way into the caves. This time, all the residents of *Beso de la Muerte* are in attendance, forming a kind of human barricade on both sides of the walkway, watching as I pass by. I pick up the whispers of the vampires among them, greeting one of their own and curious about the mortal she brings into their midst. Is she willing to share? It occurs to me that I might be delivering David like a lamb to slaughter. Something I should have thought of before.

But Culebra senses those fears. "He is under my protection," he announces in a voice loud enough for all to hear. "No harm will befall him."

It seems to work. Morbid interest dissolves once again to simple curiosity. I pass by unmolested, and we arrive at the room I remember from my last trip here.

Culebra motions to one of the gurneys and I lay David upon it. Another man joins us, his eyes on Culebra's, and without a word, he starts to work on David. He strips off my friend's shirt, covers his torso with a blanket, checks both arms. He finally looks at me, raising piercing blue eyes to meet my own.

"Do you know his blood type?" he asks in perfect, unaccented English.

I nod. I've seen it on company medical records. "O positive."

"Good." He turns to the refrigerator. "Universal. I have a good supply. Do you know how much blood he's lost?"

"No."

He draws a bag of blood from the refrigerator, sets it on the counter. He crosses to the cabinet and retrieves another bag, this time with a colorless liquid. "It's as important for us to restore his body's fluid levels as it is to restore the blood," he explains. He moves to David as he talks, arranging needles and tubes as he goes. I wince a little as he sticks one of those needles into a vein on the back of David's hand. It brings back my stay in the hospital and the beginning of all this.

But I push that out of my head. I don't want Culebra to pick up on it. Instead I watch the "doctor." He's obviously American, tall, six-something, thin. He has blond hair and blue eyes and when he reaches over David to secure one of those tubes to the side of the gurney, I see track marks on the inside of one of his arms.

Gets high on his own supply.

Explains his presence here. He may not even be a real doctor, but he seems to know what he's doing. He doesn't say anything else to me until he's finished and the two tubes running liquids into David's body are secure. Then he turns to me.

"Now it's just a matter of time. He'll either pull through or he won't."

Not very encouraging. "How long before we know?"

"A day or two. I'll keep a close eye on him."

Culebra steps beside us at David's bedside. "You have done all that you can."

Have I? David lies so still and pale on that gurney. He hasn't moved, hasn't made a sound. If he dies—

The doctor is examining his neck wounds now, and he turns to look at me. "Did you do this?"

A rush of cold fury. "No. I didn't. Can you fix it?"

He shakes his head. "Only one way to heal vampire bites. I don't have the proper equipment, so to speak."

Culebra touches my elbow.

I know immediately what he is trying to convey. A vampire bite can only be healed by another vampire. But to do that, I'd have to reopen the wound. I'd be tasting David's blood. I've only fed from other vampires before this, never a mortal.

The doctor has stepped away, giving me a clear shot of the ravages inflicted on David's neck. The wound is open, weeping, the skin torn away in jagged slices. If I don't do it, he'll bear the scars for the rest of his life—an open declaration to any other vampire that he has been fed from. Like Avery's maid.

Culebra senses my decision and motions to the doctor to follow him. He pulls the drape over the door and leaves David and I alone in the cubicle.

Can I do this?

I move to David's bedside. Physically, I know how it's done. I've done it to Avery. But with Avery it was all bound up in sex and excitement and the safety of knowing I couldn't go too far. This is David, and I don't know if the taste of mortal blood will send me into some kind of uncontrollable frenzy.

But what choice do I have? And time is running out. I have only two hours until Avery sends that car to pick me up.

And so I bend over David, gather him up and lay my lips gently against his neck. I don't have to tear at his skin; the vein is right there, close to the surface. When I break in, his blood is warm and sweet and full of the vitality of life. But I don't allow myself to drink; the puncture is only to start the healing process. My saliva mixes with his blood and tissue and I feel it begin. Sinew and vein reattach, torn skin becomes elastic. The wound closes.

When I sit back, all that's visible now is a flush of color at his neck. And even that fades as I watch. I lean down once again and kiss David's cheek.

"Are you staying the night?"

The doctor has moved back into the room. I have no idea how he knew that I had finished with David, but he is examining the wound and nodding as if finding it acceptable.

"No. I can't stay. Not tonight. But I will be back tomorrow morning."

I hope.

I feel Culebra's eyes on me. He, too, has reentered the room. I turn to face him. *We have a deal?*

He nods and holds out a hand. His grip is dry and firm.

As I return the handshake, I realize if I don't come back tomorrow, I must make arrangements for David. Culebra is the only one I can trust now.

He tilts his head as if listening to some internal dialogue. He probably is. Mine.

After a moment he says, *I will look after him if you don't return. You have a friend here in Mexico who knows him, do you not?*

A jolt. Max. But how does Culebra know?

He shrugs the question off. *If something happens, I will notify him.*

I stare at him in confusion and alarm. *Who are you?*

But he simply takes my hand again. "*Vaya con Dios,*" he says.

Go with God. I turn away. A strange benediction from a devil.

CHAPTER 38

THE DRESS IS MADE OF SILK, WOVEN SO DELI-
cately its touch is like a whisper against the skin. It
has a band of jewels that crisscross the bodice, hugging
and accenting each breast, and a sweeping skirt that falls
to the ankles. It's bright red, the color of blood, the color
of life. It's a dress that is worn naked underneath—a
dress meant to invite sex and fashioned to facilitate it.

Avery has chosen carefully. Whatever he has in mind
for tonight, there's no doubt how he envisions the evening will end. And why shouldn't he? It's the way almost every evening has ended since I first met him.

Won't he be surprised that tonight will be so different?

But this is not going to be easy. I have to scrub my
mind clear of worry for David, of this morning's ex-
plorations, of the hate hardening like concrete in the
pit of my stomach. Avery must think I'm the same
woman he bedded at the beginning of the day. If he

suspects anything else, I have no doubt he will kill me.

I run my hands along the contours of my body. I don't know how I look in Avery's masterpiece of seduction. There are no mirrors in the house, and even if there were, I couldn't use them. I can't apply makeup either, or do anything with my hair except comb it. So I use my fingers to fluff shower-wet hair and smooth gloss onto lips dry with impatience.

I want to get this over with. It's ironic that it's Avery's own strength I will use against him. He has given me his power. That's what Williams felt when I attacked him, which is why I was able to defeat him. I understand that now.

I glance at my watch. It's seven fifty. The car should be here any minute. Will Avery be inside? Somehow, I doubt it. I think he wants me to make an entrance, to glide down some gilded staircase maybe, or appear like a vision in a garden backlit by candles. He is a romantic, after all.

And I certainly fell for it.

I blow out a breath and slip into four-inch ankle-tie come-fuck-me-pumps by Manolo Blahnik. Avery thought of everything. I found these at the bottom of the garment bag.

Promptly at eight, a black Mercedes limousine turns up the driveway. I open the door to greet the driver, and no surprise, I sense immediately that he is a vampire. He must have been young when he was turned, because he looks like he's in his mid-twenties. His lean body is draped in a black tuxedo. He gives me a two-finger salute and smiles. I read in his thoughts that he likes the dress, thinks the woman in it is "hot." He doesn't seem to care that I'm reading his reactions as they occur, even the more physical ones.

The impudence of youth.

But I don't care either. Not even enough to ask how long he's been vampire. I just want him to take me to Avery.

"We're on our way," he says with a grin.

When I'm seated in the backseat, he takes his place behind the wheel. As soon as he does, his thoughts are closed to me. I look around the car, see speakers, hear the gentle shushing sound. Avery has outfitted this car with his own personal security shield, too. It's a relief, really. It means I don't have to be careful of my thoughts.

The driver turns to look back at me. "My name is Robert," he says. "And Dr. Avery told me to tell you to sit back and relax, enjoy the ride. There's chilled champagne in the refrigerator."

"Where are we going?"

Again the smile. "It's a surprise."

Then he turns his attention to the front, pushes a button that activates a privacy screen between us, and I'm left alone in the backseat with only my thoughts and a bottle of 1962 Dom Perignon for company.

The night is moonless, the air still. I watch through the windows as we head up the coast. In Del Mar, Robert turns onto a side street that winds up and away from the coastal highway and into the foothills. I lean back and sip champagne from a crystal flute, savoring the sweet excitement of the havoc I will wreak on Avery's world. The same havoc he has wrought on mine. The vision of his house in flames warms me and sustains my resolve.

But I have to temper all that out of my subconscious now. I have to turn on a different kind of flame. He has to think I'm coming to him in love, ready now to accept the life he offers. And in reality, it's not that difficult to flip that switch. After all, the passion that ignites whenever we're together burns as fiercely as the hatred inside me.

The car slows and stops in front of the gated entrance to a private club—or at least that's what the sign posted beside the guard shack says. A man in a uniform pokes his head out of the booth and nods at Robert. The gate slides open. I put the glass down and watch to see what Avery has prepared.

It's very much as I imagined.

There are luminarios lining a driveway that leads to a rambling, pillared colonial mansion. The house floats in the night like a pale ghost ship. There is no artificial light. Only candles flickering from every window. It's a fairytale setting.

Robert pulls to a stop and a liveried servant comes down the stairs to open my car door. Without a word, he steps aside as I climb out, then passes me to get to the landing and swing open the front door. I expect Avery to be waiting inside, but the only thing that greets me is soft string music floating in from open French doors just ahead. I look around but the servant is gone. I guess I'm supposed to find my own way from here.

The doors open to a rose garden, the perfume filling

the air. Still, there's no one waiting here, either, so I follow a path of flaming torches to a wide deck. It's a pool deck, the shimmering water stretching to meet the horizon in an unbroken sweep. There's a table set for two.

But still no Avery.

I approach the table, pour myself a glass of champagne—the second this evening. But this will be my last. I need to have my wits about me.

But why?

The question floats across the still night air from the far end of the pool. I turn to watch Avery as he appears at the door of a cabana and starts toward me. He has a silver vase filled with red roses in his hands.

Tonight is the perfect night to lose yourself in the moment. No thinking, no inhibitions, no "wit" required. This evening is for you.

He comes closer, his eyes sparkling in the moonlight like the flames of the candles floating in the pool. He sets the vase on the table.

I meant to have these on the table when you arrived. He holds out a finger, a drop of blood glistening in the candlelight. *But I pricked my finger on a thorn and I can't seem to get the bleeding to stop.*

I put the champagne flute down on the table and take his hand in both of my own. I raise the finger to my lips and gently suck at the wound, letting my tongue work at the cut until I feel the skin close, much the way he did with my injured leg. Much the way I did earlier with David. I keep my mind carefully closed.

When I look up at Avery, he has his eyes shut and he's swaying a little—whether to the seductive sounds of the music swelling around us or to the feel of my tongue on his skin, I can't tell. He pulls himself back when he feels my eyes on him. His smile is slow and sweet.

"You are an apt pupil," he says. "If I'm not careful, you will learn all my secrets and you will no longer need me."

I meet his eyes with my own. "I think there are still a few secrets you are keeping from me, aren't there?"

He takes a step back, but instead of answering, he focuses on the dress and me. "Beautiful. I knew it was perfect for you the moment I saw it. You are a vision, Anna."

He's all dressed up himself, in a well-cut black tuxedo. He's not wearing a tie, though, and the neck of his white silk shirt is open. The better to get right down to business.

He laughs at what I'm thinking. *Why not? We are long past the vagaries of precoital game playing, wouldn't you agree?*

I guess the honeymoon is over.

"Far from it." Avery speaks the words aloud as he dips a hand into a pocket of his jacket and pulls out a small, velvet box. "The honeymoon will never be over for us."

He holds out the box to me, a smile playing at the corners of his lips. His eyes are serious, though, as he watches me accept the box and open it.

There's a ring inside, platinum, set with a diamond solitaire that would take any living woman's breath away. I know because it elicits a gasp from me.

He's caught me completely by surprise. I expected

seduction. I expected a display of the good life vampire style. What I didn't expect was a proposal.

If that's what this is.

I look up at him, letting the confusion filter through.

He laughs. "I've rendered you speechless. A first, I think."

I hand the box back to him. "It's a beautiful ring. I can't accept it."

But he refuses to take it, pushing it back toward me. "You misunderstand. I'm not proposing. Not yet, anyway. I know it's too soon for you. But I want you to have the ring as a thank you."

A thank you? For what?

He turns away to pour himself a glass of champagne and to retrieve my glass from the edge of the table. As he hands mine back to me, he lifts his glass in a toast, his eyes bright. "To Anna. Who has brought me back from the dead. Literally. For that, no mere thank you would be sufficient."

He takes a sip and waits for me to do the same. I study him over the rim of the glass. He really believes he's in love with me. More importantly, he believes I love him, too. He believes he's won.

Suddenly it snaps into sharp focus.

Everything that has happened to me. The fire, Williams, the Revengers. Avery is behind it all.

But why?

CHAPTER 39

M Y HEART IS BEATING TOO QUICKLY, DRUM-
ming too loudly in my chest. Avery can pick up
on a thing like that. I have to calm myself, literally slow
the mad rush of my blood through my veins. He mustn't
know what I suspect.

How do I get the story from him? My first impulse,
to rip into him, doesn't seem so practical now. He has
been a vampire for three hundred years, while I, less than
a week. What worked with Williams might not work with
him. My strength comes from our union, Avery's and
mine. Am I ready to test who is the stronger?

I watch Avery.

He's busying himself with the roses, arranging them
just so in the vase. He wants everything to be perfect
tonight. He's pleased with himself, confident that he
has won me, satisfied that his life is exactly as he
wishes it to be. He is not trying to hide any of this from

me, nor is he prying into my thoughts. He is too full of self-congratulations to bother.

I move toward him, placing my glass at the table's edge. I thrust the ring box into his hand.

He takes it and raises his eyes. *You have questions for me, Anna? I sense your heart is troubled. Tell me what's wrong.*

He is being simple, direct. Let's see if he will be honest. I'll start with something he might not find threatening.

Tell me about Dena.

Avery raises an eyebrow. *My housekeeper?*

I met her today. She has marks on her neck. You have fed from her.

He nods. *Of course I have. She offered herself. Many mortals do, you know. They think it's exciting.*

You didn't hide the marks.

She didn't want me to. It's a symbol. Remember when I told you about how it could be with Max? Well, the pleasure is addicting to some and one host may not be enough.

So you had sex with her, too?

He shrugs. *Before you came into my life. I haven't touched her that way since.*

But you've taken her blood since, haven't you?

The blood was a condition of employment, the sex a perk.

That you could withdraw at any time. Did she know that? Maybe that's why she was so frightened of me. She thought I might force myself on her, feed from her, the way you did.

Avery shakes his head, an impatient little frown tugging at the corners of his mouth. *Force myself on her? I don't see it that way. She came to me of her own free will. I helped her and in turn, she helped me. She can leave my employ at any time. I don't know why she acted frightened around you. Perhaps you should ask her the next time you see her.*

His cavalier dismissal of his housekeeper's distress triggers a spark of anger in me. *I will ask her, Avery.*

The frown deepens. He speaks aloud, his voice heavy with disapproval. "Why do you persist in involving yourself with mortals? Why do you care what they want or don't want? I have tried to show you again and again that you are above all that now."

I believe that is true, Avery.

He peers at me, sudden distrust sparking in the depths of his eyes. "What are you hiding from me, Anna? What dark suspicions are you harboring? Tell me before you irreparably damage our evening."

"Will you be honest with me?"

"Haven't I always been honest?"

"No. You haven't."

He lets nothing project, no denial, no question. He simply nods his head and says, "Go on then."

I move to the other side of the table. If this is to be the showdown, I want something solid between us. "Let's start with the night of your party. You alerted the Revengers that I was coming."

"Is that a question?"

"No. The question is why? To see if I could get away? Was it some kind of performance test?"

He smiles. "If it was, you passed, didn't you? You got away."

"And came straight back to you. Was that the idea? Was that the reason you had my house burned down, too? To assure I would be dependent on you?"

He doesn't respond, his mind as blank and impenetrable as his expression.

"You didn't have to do that, you know. The bond between us had already been forged. My home was special to me. My grandparents raised my mother there. Now I have nothing left of that life. It was a stupid, pointless, hurtful thing to do."

Avery stirs a little, eyes flashing in the candlelight, but still, he says nothing, lets no emotion filter into his thoughts.

It's disconcerting, but I've come this far. I may as well press on.

"Then there's Donaldson and *Beso de la Muerte*. A very good distraction. It's taken me a while to figure that one out, but I think I have it now. You killed him, didn't you? And you wounded me in order to slow me down so you could get home before I did. I think you planned to kill him *before* I found out he knew nothing about David or the fire, but you weren't quite quick enough. Still, there must be something else about Donaldson that you didn't want me to know. Like maybe, your connection to him? He hardly seemed the type to seek out vampires. He had a family that, judging from the pictures I found at the cave, he still cared about. Yet, he became a vampire, and you called him a rogue. How does that happen? Was he your rogue?"

This time, Avery allows himself a smile. "You are a wonder, Anna, do you know that?" He sips delicately at the glass in his hand, his eyes locked with mine. "If I'd had any idea how smart you are, or how intuitive, I might just have killed you in the hospital. Perhaps I should have."

"Your mistake, I agree. Will you answer my question?"

He blows out an impatient sigh. "I turned Donaldson. He was a fussy, irritating little man who happened to stumble on an impropriety in one of the hospital accounts. He was doing an audit for his company. He made the mistake of coming to me about it. I convinced him he had more to gain by looking the other way. When he objected, I set up the bookkeeping discrepancy in his own firm. I showed him how easy it was for one with computer savvy to set up such things. When his boss found out about it, Donaldson came over to my side very quickly. He didn't want to go to jail. I gave him immortality and the hospital problem disappeared. He was supposed to leave the country right away. How was I to know he had such a dark nature? It happens sometimes. He found he liked the killing. He left his family to protect them, the last decent thing he did."

He's still smiling at me, but there's no warmth now. He's watching me the same way a cat might watch a mouse, and he waits for my next move with the same placid feline patience. He's not the least bit afraid.

I rest the palms of my hands on the table and lean forward to continue.

"And what about Williams, what he said to me and

what happened after? It wasn't me he needed to hide from, was it? He was afraid of you and what you might do when you found out what he told me. He was afraid of your power. Not mine. He retreated because he thought you and I were in league and that somehow threatened him. I still don't understand it."

I look into Avery's dark eyes. "But you aren't going to explain it, are you?"

Surprisingly, he responds. "You would not understand the balance of power between old-soul vampires in a community. Not yet. I think perhaps now you never will."

"That's it? That's all you're going to say?"

A long moment passes. I have to fight back anger and frustration and regain my composure before I broach the subject most important to me—David.

His sharp eyes detect a shift in my expression; his mind probes into my subconscious. "You are very good at hiding your thoughts from me, Anna," he says softly. "But there is something more you want from me."

He's turned his back to me, champagne glass in one hand, the velvet ring box in the other, staring out at the horizon. His shoulders slump a little and he adds, "I'm sorry it's come to this. I had such hopes for us." He fingers the box. "The stone in this ring belonged to my mother. In the past, it's been worn by women, mortal women, good women. When I met you, though, I knew you were the last one destined to wear it. For all eternity."

He slips the box back into his jacket pocket. "But you can't let go. I read it in your heart. Your home. Your friends. Even when I strip them away, you refuse to let go."

I don't move from my place. I'm sure now that Avery knows what I've done. How he will react may determine whether I survive this or not.

He places the glass down on the table. "This is all about your friend, David, isn't it?"

Yes.

He turns to look at me. The candlelight on his face reflects, in icy radiance, an expression both hostile and derisive. He opens his mind and draws me in, daring me physically to come closer.

But I keep my distance because what I feel emanating from him is both frightening and malignant.

There's nothing soft or loving or forgiving left in his heart or his attitude toward me. Those feelings are erased by the enormity of cold fury.

"You found him," he says simply.

Only his eyes blaze with contempt, flashing the danger.

He's letting me into his thoughts to scare me, and it works.

CHAPTER 40

AVERY HAS THE ABILITY TO STAND SO STILL one might think he was made of iron or steel, and at the same time radiate energy so great it stops your heart and freezes your ability to think or to feel anything except sheer terror. I felt it yesterday in the attic.

I feel it again now.

I have to fight it, calm myself, swallow back the fear and stop the pounding of my blood. He may be older than I am, but I've proven myself with Donaldson and Williams. I have used the knowledge passed to me through Avery's own blood, and I can do it again.

He smiles as he reads all this in my thoughts and interprets the rigid bearing of my body. "You are ready to fight me."

It's not a question, nor is it a simple statement. He's making a joke, laughing at my audacity. The fact that he's chosen to vocalize this emphasizes his contempt for the presumption.

If I have to. I want you to explain why you did it. You knew how important David is to me. My house was a thing. You took that without a second thought, but David is a person—a human being. You had no right—

Before my eyes register the movement, before I can move away, he's come around the table and is standing so close, I feel his breath on my cheek. "Don't speak to me with your mind. You are so tied to mortals, you denigrate the vampire heritage. Use your voice. It's all *you* have a right to."

He's leaning over me, his mouth at my neck. He's gnashing his teeth as if fighting to keep from tearing my throat out. I have to wonder why he doesn't.

He pulls back an inch. "I thought you wanted answers. You've given me a great deal of pleasure in the last few days. I will tell you what you want to know before you die. But," he leans in again, "first you must tell me. Where did you take David?"

Now it's my turn to let the anger come through. Stubbornly, I send my thoughts out to him. *He is safe. And protected. You can't get to him no matter what happens to me.*

"Oh, you think not?" His hands encircle my waist, pull me close. "I will take the information I need. I will take it with the last drop of your blood."

Every nerve in my body tenses. The adrenaline turns my blood to fire as I prepare to fight. Then I remember Williams. I clear my mind, center myself, let my muscles relax for just the instant it takes to catch Avery slightly off guard. He expected me to lunge or jerk away. Instead, I lean in toward him and bring my hands up to rest on his chest. Before he can react, I use every ounce of strength to hurl him away.

He flies back, crashing into one of the wooden patio chairs dotting the pool deck. It splinters under his weight. His eyes widen, then flash. Suddenly, he's on his feet again, a movement so quick it's like an illusion. One second he's on the ground, the next he's coming toward me.

"Very good. I see how you got the better of Williams. Well, I won't make the mistake of underestimating your strength again. Let's see if you are as mentally powerful."

He stops a foot from me, and without warning, his eyes change. I watch transfixed as the pupils elongate, like a cat's, and the color loses depth and becomes translucent. He's using them to bore into my head, to fill my mind with numbing pain that roots me to the spot. I can't even lower my eyelids or raise my hands to ward it off. It's like a laser cutting into my thoughts, seeking out the information and excising it with white-hot efficiency.

Then it stops.

Avery smiles. His eyes morph back into human ones. "*Beso de la Muerte*. Very resourceful."

No.

"And you've enlisted the help of Culebra. Well. He may prove to be a formidable adversary. But not an insurmountable one."

Leave David out of this.

He starts to circle. "Leave him out? He's the reason

I've lost you. I should have simply killed him and been done with it."

Then what? Would you have gone after my parents next, and Max?

"If necessary. Frankly, I thought by this time you would have realized that mortals are food to us, like cattle, nothing more. I chose David to make the point because he is a friend, not a blood tie or an involvement. Once he was out of your life, you could move on. He seemed the most expendable."

Expendable?

"An object lesson. You would have grieved for him, but that would have passed. Like your home, another tie to your life as a mortal would have been removed. Just as you came to me after your confrontation with the Revengers, and again after the fire, you would have turned to me for solace, and I would have reminded you how temporary human attachments are. I told you once before, it's a lesson best learned at the beginning."

And then I would have been all yours.

"You were all mine. You needed very little persuasion to fall under my spell."

He's still circling, toying with me again like a cat with a mouse, projecting a smug haughtiness that lets me know how insignificant I had proved to be in the scheme of things.

Your spell? Was it a trick, then? The way you made me feel?

He snorts and throws up a hand. "Spell? Merely a turn of phrase. I needed no spell to win you. You are a very sexual woman, Anna. I introduced you to the most pleasurable coupling of all—the mingling of body and mind and blood—and you responded. Why do you think I chose David and not Max? I knew with Max it would be only a matter of time before you found sex with him unfulfilling. Even if you fed from him, it would not be the same. David, on the other hand, holds you in the stronger grip of friendship. I needed to loosen that grip."

His words prick at my conscience because I know he is right. I wanted to believe Avery somehow worked a spell on me that I was powerless to resist. But the truth is, I found him the most exciting man I'd ever been with. Even now, the memory of how it felt sends an involuntary thrill up my spine.

He laughs at my reaction. "You see?"

No. I can fight it. I must. I shake my head, willing the feelings to pass. He's misjudged me. Sex would never be enough to make me forget the rest of what he's done. And I would have found out, one way or the other. He should have let me choose my own path.

Avery picks up on my last thought.

"You sound like a whiny child," he says with another wave of his hand. "Let me choose my own path. Why would I? I've lived three hundred years on my own terms. I've always dictated what choices my consorts have, not the other way around."

That ignites a spark within me. "Which might explain why Marianna killed herself."

He reacts as if I'd slapped his face. He rears back, teeth flashing, eyes sparking with fury. "Don't mention her name."

Have I touched a nerve, Avery? What did you want Marianna to do that drove her to take her own life? Did you try to turn her? Did you force yourself on her like you did Dena? Did she refuse to let you take her blood?

Avery lunges at me, bending me back over the table before I can counter his thrust. "I grow weary of this conversation," he hisses in my ear. "It's time to end it."

His teeth grab the skin just at my jugular and start to rip it away. I work an arm between his face and my chest and heave him back. He doesn't fall completely away, but his body gives enough for me to leverage myself with one hand on his chin and the other on his chest. I push with all my strength, keeping those snapping teeth away from my neck. But I can't reach his neck, either, so we're caught in a macabre embrace.

Anna, look at me.

But I press my eyes shut. I know what he's trying to do. *No.*

Open your eyes. You can't resist. You know that.

But I do resist, though I don't know how long I'll be able to hold him off. He's wearing away at my strength and resolve. He's in my head, telling me to let go, telling me how easy it will be and how peaceful when it's over.

No. I won't let him kill me.

I reach deep into myself and channel all my anger toward him for a final thrust. It's a feeling that starts in the pit of my stomach, a fury that gains momentum and power until it explodes outward. Suddenly, it's Avery, not me, bent over that table. I grab his arms and fling him onto the ground, bent on finishing it. He fights back, sending me flying off him and crashing into a chair. I feel it disintegrate into a hundred pieces beneath me. But before I can regain balance, he's on top of me, holding me down. His face moves closer, a smile twisting his mouth.

It would have been so good, Anna. I waited so long for a worthy companion. I reveled in finding you, in showing you what could be. I loved you. I loved you.

His anguish burns through me, first the love, then the hatred. It sears into my brain, cuts nerve endings and flays my flesh. I feel it stripping away. He isn't using his teeth; he isn't draining my blood. The intensity of his hatred peels my skin as if with a knife. I'm on fire. He wants me to suffer before he ends it.

Frantically, I feel around for something, anything, to use as a weapon. My hand closes around a wooden spool, the armrest of the chair I'm resting upon. I snatch it up, grasp it with both hands, and with a single motion, plunge it into Avery's back.

There's a moment when all time stops. Avery's face hovers above me. His eyes reflect surprise, then sadness. A pitiful howl erupts from deep inside him, and in the next instant, he's gone.

CHAPTER 41

I DON'T KNOW HOW LONG I LIE THERE, ALONE,
exhausted, afraid, the stake still clutched in my hands.

Finally, I hold up a hand before my face. I expect to
see blood and exposed bone and sinew. Instead my arm
is whole, unmarked. It was a mind trick, the flayed skin,
the burning.

It's over.

Avery is gone. Disappeared. As if he never existed.
My heart thuds a dirge in the center of my chest. It
could have been me. Should have been me.

I can't figure out why it wasn't.

The answer comes from a now familiar voice.

*Avery was careless. He underestimated you. And your
loyalty to your friend.*

I look around slowly, too weary to be startled. *Casper?
Are you all right?*

I gather strength, pull myself into a sitting position.

My hand goes to my neck. There's some blood, but Avery never got a real hold. Thankfully. *Where are you? Why didn't you help me?*

Not allowed.

Then at least show yourself.

Maybe another time. I'm just here to check that you are all right. Robert is out back with the car to take you home.

Home. I shake my head sadly. *I don't have a home.*

Sure you do. Avery's place is yours now.

I sniff. *I don't think so.*

But it's true. You vanquished an old soul in defense of your own life. All his possessions are yours.

What if I don't want them?

Up to you. But before you dismiss it out of hand, think of how much good you could do with that kind of wealth. You could help a lot of people.

I can't think about it now.

No rush. You have all the time in the world.

CHAPTER 42

IDON'T REMEMBER THE RIDE TO THE LOFT OR letting myself into David's or falling as if dead onto the couch. When I awaken, I simply find myself there, bone weary, despite having slept for ten hours. I drag myself into the bathroom, stripping off Avery's dress. Balling it up, I stuff the thing into the trash. Then I take a long, hot shower. Lately it seems I can't get the water hot enough. Still, even the scalding heat doesn't quite wash away the feel of Avery's hands on my body.

I'm not sure anything will.

After, I pull on the only clothes I can find in David's room that fit—a pair of Gloria's designer sweats and a Broncos sweatshirt—and haul myself down to the garage to get the Hummer.

Max is sitting by David's bedside when I get to *Beso de la Muerte*. I'm not even that surprised to see him.

After what I've been through the last few days, it will take a lot to surprise me from now on.

David is asleep, tubes still attached, but his breathing is deep and regular.

Max reads the question in my eyes and says, "He's going to be all right. The doc says he'll be out for another day or two, but when he awakens, he'll be as good as new."

He gets up and puts an arm around my shoulders. "Culebra told me you've had quite a time of it."

I don't respond to that. I don't know how. Instead I ask, "What are you doing here?"

He gives me a kiss on the forehead. "I guess you haven't had a chance to see a paper in the last couple of days. The operation is over. I'm just here to clean up a few loose ends."

"And you know about this place?"

He nods.

"*All* about this place?"

He shrugs. "If you mean do I know that there are some rather interesting specimens that occasionally use *Beso de la Muerte* as a hideout, the answer is yes."

I'm wondering if he's going to ask me how I found out about it when Culebra joins us.

He bends at the waist in a little bow toward me. "Anna. How nice to see you. I explained to Max that you followed Donaldson down here and that David was injured trying to apprehend him. I'm afraid it's probably the last we've seen of that one."

I send him a quick thank you, which he acknowledges

with a smile. Then I turn to Max. "So, you two were working together?"

"Culebra has helped us on several projects."

"Only, of course, when Max's interest doesn't conflict with mine," Culebra adds.

"Of course," Max responds. Then he gestures toward David. "I have to get back to San Diego. Will you be staying here with David?"

"For a little while. I'll bring him home as soon as he can travel."

He touches my cheek. "I heard about the fire. Where are you living?"

"At David's for now. Then, I'll probably move home with my folks until the cottage is rebuilt."

He nods and after exchanging a few words with Culebra in Spanish, he kisses my cheek and is gone.

Culebra raises an eyebrow at me. "You aren't staying at—" he starts to say "Avery's," then corrects himself, "Your other place?"

I shake my head. "I don't think I could stand to be there. I don't know what I'm going to do about that yet." I narrow my eyes and look hard at him. "How do you know so much? Are you reading all that in my head?"

He laughs. "It's a blessing and a curse."

"Do you really think David will be all right?"

"He'll be fine. He won't remember anything that happened to him at Avery's. You'll have to come up with a story about how he was injured. Other than that, you'll have your friend back good as new."

"Maybe it would be better if I took him home before

he fully regains consciousness. I don't know how I would explain it if he woke up here."

Culebra nods. "Come back tomorrow afternoon. He will be able to travel then."

"You're sure?"

He taps the side of his head. "I'm always sure."

Must be nice.

I start to go and then I remember. *I owe you a favor.*

He smiles. *I haven't forgotten. And there's no hurry to collect, now, is there?*

No, I guess there isn't.

AFTERWORD

DAVID DID RECOVER AND JUST AS CULEBRA predicted, didn't remember anything of his kidnapping or the ordeal in Avery's hidden room. I made up a story about his getting bumped by a car while we were chasing Donaldson. I told him he fell and hit his head on a curb, joked with him that it was becoming a habit. He accepted it grumpily, especially when the "insurance" check came from the errant driver.

Williams had a miraculous recovery from his "stroke," too, on the same evening, coincidentally, that Avery was killed. We haven't spoken yet, though he has tried to get in touch with me. I'm not ready to face him yet. But I will be. He has answers I need.

I don't know what I'm going to do about my "inheritance." I've closed the house for now. The hospital thinks Avery has taken a sabbatical after long years of dedicated service. They were notified of his decision via computer. They were understandably sorry to see him go, but knew he could use a rest. He had done good work for the hospital, regardless of the reason, and that's the way he will be remembered.

I let Dena go with a healthy severance check from my own account. She was neither relieved nor disappointed. I told her what she could do to rid herself of the bite marks, but I'm not sure she'll do it. She didn't ask me for help and I didn't offer. In spite of how she acted around me, I have the feeling Avery was right. She found life with him exciting.

I don't know what direction my life will take now that I'm on my own. David and I are back at work. He thinks nothing has changed. And so far, it hasn't. So far, the hunger hasn't hit.

But I know it will. It's my nature now. Casper "drops in" every now and then and assures me I will be able to handle it. I have so many questions for him, but he won't reveal himself. I don't know why. After what happened with Avery, maybe that's a good thing. Maybe I'm not strong enough yet.

In a few days, though, it will have been a month since I last fed.

The hunger is coming.

I feel it.

I can only hope Casper is right.

Jeanne C. Stein was raised and educated in San Diego, the setting for her Anna Strong series. She now lives with her husband outside Denver, Colorado, where, besides working on her books, she edits a newsletter for a beer importer and manages to work in weekly kickboxing classes to stay in shape.

Coming Soon!

THE ULTIMATE IN
SCIENCE FICTION AND FANTASY!

From magical tales of distant worlds to stories of
technological advances beyond the grasp of man, Penguin has
everything you need to stretch your imagination to its limits.

penguin.com

ACE
Get the latest information on favorites like
William Gibson, T.A. Barron, Brian Jacques,
Ursula Le Guin, Sharon Shinn, and Charlaine Harris,
as well as updates on the best new authors.

ROC
Escape with Harry Turtledove, Anne Bishop,
S.M. Stirling, Simon Green, Chris Bunch, Jim Butcher,
E.E. Knight, and many others—plus news on the
latest and hottest in science fiction and fantasy.

DAW
Mercedes Lackey, Kristen Britain, Tanya Huff,
Tad Williams, C.J. Cherryh, and many more—
DAW has something to satisfy the cravings of any
science fiction and fantasy lover.
Also visit dawbooks.com.

*Get the best of science fiction and fantasy
at your fingertips!*